The Tremendous Adventures of Major Gahagan by Thackeray

The great author of Vanity Fair and The Luck Of Barry Lyndon was born in India in 1811.

At age 5 his father died and his mother sent him back to England. His education was of the best but he himself seemed unable to apply his talents to a rigorous work ethic.

However, once he harnessed his talents the works flowed in novels, articles, short stories, sketches and lectures.

Sadly, his personal life was rather more difficult. After a few years of marriage his wife began to suffer from depression and over the years became detached from reality. Thackeray himself suffered from ill health later in his life and the one pursuit that kept him moving forward was that of writing. In his life time, he was placed second only to Dickens. High praise indeed.

Index of Contents
CHAPTER I - "TRUTH IS STRANGE, STRANGER THAN FICTION."
CHAPTER II - ALLYGHUR AND LASWAREE
CHAPTER III - A PEEP INTO SPAIN—ACCOUNT OF THE ORIGIN AND SERVICES OF THE AHMEDNUGGAR IRREGULARS
CHAPTER IV - THE INDIAN CAMP—THE SORTIE FROM THE FORT
CHAPTER V - THE ISSUE OF MY INTERVIEW WITH MY WIFE
CHAPTER VI - FAMINE IN THE GARRISON
CHAPTER VII - THE ESCAPE
CHAPTER VIII - THE CAPTIVE
CHAPTER IX - SURPRISE OF FUTTYGHUR
WILLIAM MAKEPEACE THACKERAY – A SHORT BIOGRAPHY
WILLIAM MAKEPEACE THACKERAY – A CONCISE BIBLIOGRAPHY

CHAPTER I

"TRUTH IS STRANGE, STRANGER THAN FICTION."

I think it but right that in making my appearance before the public I should at once acquaint them with my titles and name. My card, as I leave it at the houses of the nobility, my friends, is as follows:

MAJOR GOLIAH O'GRADY GAHAGAN, H.E.I.C.S., Commanding Battalion of Irregular Horse, AHMEDNUGGAR.

Seeing, I say, this simple visiting ticket, the world will avoid any of those awkward mistakes as to my person, which have been so frequent of late. There has been no end to the blunders regarding this humble title of mine, and the confusion thereby created. When I published my volume of poems, for instance, the Morning Post newspaper remarked "that the Lyrics of the Heart, by Miss Gahagan, may be ranked among the sweetest flowrets of the present spring season." The Quarterly Review, commenting upon my "Observations on the Pons Asinorum" (4to, London, 1836), called me "Doctor Gahagan," and so on. It was time to put an end to these mistakes, and I have taken the above simple remedy.

I was urged to it by a very exalted personage. Dining in August last at the palace of the T-l-r-es at Paris, the lovely young Duch- ss of Orl-ns (who, though she does not speak English, understands it as well as I do), said to me in the softest Teutonic, "Lieber Herr Major, haben sie den Ahmednuggarischen-jager-battalion gelassen?" "Warum denn?" said I, quite astonished at her R-l H- ss's question. The P-cess then spoke of some trifle from my pen, which was simply signed Goliah Gahagan.

There was, unluckily, a dead silence as H.R.H. put this question.

"Comment donc?" said H.M. Lo-is Ph-l-ppe, looking gravely at Count Mole; "le cher Major a quitte l'armee! Nicolas donc sera maitre de l'Inde!" H. M- and the Pr. M-n-ster pursued their conversation in a low tone, and left me, as may be imagined, in a dreadful state of confusion. I blushed and stuttered, and murmured out a few incoherent words to explain—but it would not do—I could not recover my equanimity during the course of the dinner; and while endeavouring to help an English duke, my neighbour, to poulet a l'Austerlitz, fairly sent seven mushrooms and three large greasy croutes over his whiskers and shirt-frill. Another laugh at my expense. "Ah! M. le Major," said the Q- of the B-lg-ns, archly, "vous n'aurez jamais votre brevet de Colonel." Her M-y's joke will be better understood when I state that his Grace is the brother of a Minister.

I am not at liberty to violate the sanctity of private life, by mentioning the names of the parties concerned in this little anecdote. I only wish to have it understood that I am a gentleman, and live at least in DECENT society. Verbum sat.

But to be serious. I am obliged always to write the name of Goliah in full, to distinguish me from my brother, Gregory Gahagan, who was also a Major (in the King's service), and whom I killed in a duel, as the public most likely knows. Poor Greg! a very trivial dispute was the cause of our quarrel, which never would have originated but for the similarity of our names. The circumstance was this: I had been lucky enough to render the Nawaub of Lucknow some trifling service (in the notorious affair of Choprasjee Muckjee), and his Highness sent down a gold toothpick-case directed to Captain G. Gahagan, which I of course thought was for me: my brother madly claimed it; we fought, and the consequence was, that in about three minutes he received a slash in the right side (cut 6), which effectually did his business:- he was a good swordsman enough—I was THE BEST in the universe. The most ridiculous part of the affair is, that the toothpick-case was his, after all—he had left it on the Nawaub's table at tiffin. I can't conceive what madness prompted him to fight about such a paltry bauble; he had much better have yielded it at once, when he saw I was determined to have it. From this slight specimen of my adventures, the reader will perceive that my life has been one of no ordinary interest; and, in fact, I may say that I have led a more remarkable life than any man in the service—I have been at more pitched battles, led more forlorn hopes, had more success among the fair sex, drunk harder, read more, been a handsomer man than any officer now serving Her Majesty.

When I first went to India in 1802, I was a raw cornet of seventeen, with blazing red hair, six feet four in height, athletic at all kinds of exercises, owing money to my tailor and everybody else who would trust me, possessing an Irish brogue, and my full pay of 120l. a year. I need not say that with all these advantages I did that which a number of clever fellows have done before me—I fell in love, and proposed to marry immediately.

But how to overcome the difficulty? It is true that I loved Julia Jowler—loved her to madness; but her father intended her for a Member of Council at least, and not for a beggarly Irish ensign. It was, however, my fate to make the passage to India (on board of the "Samuel Snob" East Indiaman, Captain Duffy) with this lovely creature, and my misfortune instantaneously to fall in love with her. We were not out of the Channel before I adored her, worshipped the deck which she trod upon, kissed a thousand times the cuddy-chair on which she used to sit. The same madness fell on every man in the ship. The two mates fought about her at the Cape; the surgeon, a sober pious Scotchman, from disappointed affection, took so dreadfully to drinking as to threaten spontaneous combustion; and old Colonel Lilywhite, carrying his wife and seven daughters to Bengal, swore that he would have a divorce from Mrs. L., and made an attempt at suicide; the captain himself told me, with tears in his eyes, that he hated his hitherto-adored Mrs. Duffy, although he had had nineteen children by her.

We used to call her the witch—there was magic in her beauty and in her voice. I was spell-bound when I looked at her, and stark staring mad when she looked at me! O lustrous black eyes!—O glossy night-black ringlets!—O lips!—O dainty frocks of white muslin!—O tiny kid slippers!—though old and gouty, Gahagan sees you still! I recollect, off Ascension, she looked at me in her particular way one day at dinner, just as I happened to be blowing on a piece of scalding hot green fat. I was stupefied at once—I thrust the entire morsel (about half a pound) into my mouth. I made no attempt to swallow, or to masticate it, but left it there for many minutes, burning, burning! I had no skin to my palate for seven weeks after, and lived on rice-water during the rest of the voyage. The anecdote is trivial, but it shows the power of Julia Jowler over me.

The writers of marine novels have so exhausted the subject of storms, shipwrecks, mutinies, engagements, sea-sickness, and so forth, that (although I have experienced each of these in many varieties) I think it quite unnecessary to recount such trifling adventures; suffice it to say, that during our five months' trajet, my mad passion for Julia daily increased; so did the captain's and the surgeon's; so did Colonel Lilywhite's; so did the doctor's, the mate's—that of most part of the passengers, and a considerable number of the crew. For myself, I swore—ensign as I was—I would win her for my wife; I vowed that I would make her glorious with my sword—that as soon as I had made a favourable impression on my commanding officer (which I did not doubt to create), I would lay open to him the state of my affections, and demand his daughter's hand. With such sentimental outpourings did our voyage continue and conclude.

We landed at the Sunderbunds on a grilling hot day in December 1802, and then for the moment Julia and I separated. She was carried off to her papa's arms in a palankeen, surrounded by at least forty hookahbadars; whilst the poor cornet, attended but by two dandies and a solitary beasty (by which unnatural name these blackamoors are called), made his way humbly to join the regiment at headquarters.

The -'th Regiment of Bengal Cavalry, then under the command of Lieut.-Colonel Julius Jowler, C.B., was known throughout Asia and Europe by the proud title of the Bundelcund Invincibles—so great was its character for bravery, so remarkable were its services in that delightful district of India. Major Sir George Gutch was next in command, and Tom Thrupp, as kind a fellow as ever ran a Mahratta through the body, was second Major. We were on the eve of that remarkable war which was speedily to spread throughout the whole of India, to call forth the valour of a Wellesley, and the indomitable gallantry of a Gahagan; which was illustrated by our victories at Ahmednuggar (where I was the first over the barricade at the storming of the Pettah); at Argaum, where I slew with my own sword twenty-three matchlock-men, and cut a dromedary in two; and by that terrible day of Assaye, where Wellesley would have been beaten but for me—me alone: I headed nineteen charges of cavalry, took (aided by only four men of my own troop) seventeen field-pieces, killing the scoundrelly French artillerymen; on that day I had eleven elephants shot under me, and carried away Scindiah's nose- ring with a pistol-ball. Wellesley is a Duke and a Marshal, I but a simple Major of Irregulars. Such is fortune and war! But my feelings carry me away from my narrative, which had better proceed with more order.

On arriving, I say, at our barracks at Dum Dum, I for the first time put on the beautiful uniform of the Invincibles: a light blue swallow-tailed jacket with silver lace and wings, ornamented with about 3,000 sugar-loaf buttons, rhubarb-coloured leather inexpressibles (tights), and red morocco boots with silver spurs and tassels, set off to admiration the handsome persons of the officers of our corps. We wore powder in those days; and a regulation pigtail of seventeen inches, a brass helmet surrounded by leopard skin, with a bearskin top and a horsetail feather, gave the head a fierce and chivalrous appearance, which is far more easily imagined than described.

Attired in this magnificent costume, I first presented myself before Colonel Jowler. He was habited in a manner precisely similar, but not being more than five feet in height, and weighing at least fifteen stone, the dress he wore did not become him quite so much as slimmer and taller men. Flanked by his tall Majors, Thrupp and Gutch, he looked like a stumpy skittle-ball between two attenuated skittles. The plump little Colonel received me with vast cordiality, and I speedily became a prime favourite with himself and the other officers of the corps. Jowler was the most hospitable of men; and gratifying my appetite and my love together, I continually partook of his dinners, and feasted on the sweet presence of Julia.

I can see now, what I would not and could not perceive in those early days, that this Miss Jowler—on whom I had lavished my first and warmest love, whom I had endowed with all perfection and purity— was no better than a little impudent flirt, who played with my feelings, because during the monotony of a sea voyage she had no other toy to play with; and who deserted others for me, and me for others, just as her whim or her interest might guide her. She had not been three weeks at headquarters when half the regiment was in love with her. Each and all of the candidates had some favour to boast of, or some encouraging hopes on which to build. It was the scene of the "Samuel Snob" over again, only heightened in interest by a number of duels. The following list will give the reader a notion of some of them:-

1. Cornet Gahagan . . . Ensign Hicks, of the Sappers and Miners. Hicks received a ball in his jaw, and was half choked by a quantity of carroty whisker forced down his throat with the ball.

2. Captain Macgillicuddy, B.N.I. Cornet Gahagan. I was run through the body, but the sword passed between the ribs, and injured me very slightly.

3. Captain Macgillicuddy, B.N.I. Mr. Mulligatawny, B.C.S., Deputy- Assistant Vice Sub-Controller of the Boggleywollah Indigo grounds, Ramgolly branch.

Macgillicuddy should have stuck to sword's play, and he might have come off in his second duel as well as in his first; as it was, the civilian placed a ball and a part of Mac's gold repeater in his stomach. A remarkable circumstance attended this shot, an account of which I sent home to the "Philosophical Transactions:" the surgeon had extracted the ball, and was going off, thinking that all was well, when the gold repeater struck thirteen in poor Macgillicuddy's abdomen. I suppose that the works must have been disarranged in some way by the bullet, for the repeater was one of Barraud's, never known to fail before, and the circumstance occurred at seven o'clock.

I could continue, almost ad infinitum, an account of the wars which this Helen occasioned, but the above three specimens will, I should think, satisfy the peaceful reader. I delight not in scenes of blood, Heaven knows, but I was compelled in the course of a few weeks, and for the sake of this one woman, to fight nine duels myself, and I know that four times as many more took place concerning her.

I forgot to say that Jowler's wife was a half-caste woman, who had been born and bred entirely in India, and whom the Colonel had married from the house of her mother, a native. There were some singular rumours abroad regarding this latter lady's history: it was reported that she was the daughter of a native Rajah, and had been carried off by a poor English subaltern in Lord Clive's time. The young man was killed very soon after, and left his child with its mother. The black Prince forgave his daughter and bequeathed to her a handsome sum of money. I suppose that it was on this account that Jowler married Mrs. J., a creature who had not, I do believe, a Christian name, or a single Christian quality: she was a hideous, bloated, yellow creature, with a beard, black teeth, and red eyes: she was fat, lying, ugly, and stingy—she hated and was hated by all the world, and by her jolly husband as devoutly as by any other. She did not pass a month in the year with him, but spent most of her time with her native friends. I wonder how she could have given birth to so lovely a creature as her daughter. This woman was of course with the Colonel when Julia arrived, and the spice of the devil in her daughter's composition was most carefully nourished and fed by her. If Julia had been a flirt before, she was a downright jilt now; she set the whole cantonment by the ears; she made wives jealous and husbands miserable; she caused all those duels of which I have discoursed already, and yet such was the fascination of THE WITCH that I still thought her an angel. I made court to the nasty mother in order to be near the daughter; and I listened untiringly to Jowler's interminable dull stories, because I was occupied all the time in watching the graceful movements of Miss Julia.

But the trumpet of war was soon ringing in our ears; and on the battle-field Gahagan is a man! The Bundelcund Invincibles received orders to march, and Jowler, Hector-like, donned his helmet and prepared to part from his Andromache. And now arose his perplexity: what must be done with his daughter, his Julia? He knew his wife's peculiarities of living, and did not much care to trust his daughter to her keeping; but in vain he tried to find her an asylum among the respectable ladies of his regiment. Lady Gutch offered to receive her, but would have nothing to do with Mrs. Jowler; the surgeon's wife, Mrs. Sawbone, would have neither mother nor daughter: there was no help for it, Julia and her mother must have a house together, and Jowler knew that his wife would fill it with her odious blackamoor friends.

I could not, however, go forth satisfied to the campaign until I learned from Julia my fate. I watched twenty opportunities to see her alone, and wandered about the Colonel's bungalow as an informer does about a public-house, marking the incomings and the outgoings of the family, and longing to seize the moment when Miss Jowler, unbiassed by her mother or her papa, might listen, perhaps, to my eloquence, and melt at the tale of my love.

But it would not do—old Jowler seemed to have taken all of a sudden to such a fit of domesticity, that there was no finding him out of doors, and his rhubarb-coloured wife (I believe that her skin gave the first idea of our regimental breeches), who before had been gadding ceaselessly abroad, and poking her broad nose into every menage in the cantonment, stopped faithfully at home with her spouse. My only chance was to beard the old couple in their den, and ask them at once for their cub.

So I called one day at tiffin:- old Jowler was always happy to have my company at this meal; it amused him, he said, to see me drink Hodgson's pale ale (I drank two hundred and thirty-four dozen the first year I was in Bengal)—and it was no small piece of fun, certainly, to see old Mrs. Jowler attack the currie-bhaut;—she was exactly the colour of it, as I have already the honour to remark, and she swallowed the mixture with a gusto which was never equalled, except by my poor friend Dando a propos d'huitres. She consumed the first three platefuls with a fork and spoon, like a Christian; but as she warmed to her work, the old hag would throw away her silver implements, and dragging the dishes towards her, go to work with her hands, flip the rice into her mouth with her fingers, and stow away a quantity of eatables sufficient for a sepoy company. But why do I diverge from the main point of my story?

Julia, then, Jowler, and Mrs. J., were at luncheon; the dear girl was in the act to sabler a glass of Hodgson as I entered. "How do you do, Mr. Gagin?" said the old hag, leeringly. "Eat a bit o' currie-bhaut,"—and she thrust the dish towards me, securing a heap as it passed. "What! Gagy my boy, how do, how do?" said the fat Colonel. "What! run through the body?—got well again—have some Hodgson—run through your body too!"—and at this, I may say, coarse joke (alluding to the fact that in these hot climates the ale oozes out as it were from the pores of the skin) old Jowler laughed: a host of swarthy chobdars, kitmatgars, sices, consomahs, and bobbychies laughed too, as they provided me, unasked, with the grateful fluid. Swallowing six tumblers of it, I paused nervously for a moment, and then said -

"Bobbachy, consomah, ballybaloo hoga."

The black ruffians took the hint, and retired.

"Colonel and Mrs. Jowler," said I solemnly, "we are alone; and you, Miss Jowler, you are alone too; that is—I mean—I take this opportunity to—(another glass of ale, if you please)—to express, once for all, before departing on a dangerous campaign"—(Julia turned pale)—"before entering, I say, upon a war which may stretch in the dust my high-raised hopes and me, to express my hopes while life still remains to me, and to declare in the face of heaven, earth, and Colonel Jowler, that I love you, Julia!" The Colonel, astonished, let fall a steel fork, which stuck quivering for some minutes in the calf of my leg; but I heeded not the paltry interruption. "Yes, by yon bright heaven," continued I, "I love you, Julia! I respect my commander, I esteem your excellent and beauteous mother: tell me, before I leave you, if I may hope for a return of my affection. Say that you love me, and I will do such deeds in this coming war, as shall make you proud of the name of your Gahagan."

The old woman, as I delivered these touching words, stared, snapped, and ground her teeth, like an enraged monkey. Julia was now red, now white; the Colonel stretched forward, took the fork out of the calf of my leg, wiped it, and then seized a bundle of letters which I had remarked by his side.

"A cornet!" said he, in a voice choking with emotion; "a pitiful beggarly Irish cornet aspire to the hand of Julia Jowler! Gag— Gahagan, are you mad, or laughing at us? Look at these letters, young man—at these letters, I say—one hundred and twenty-four epistles from every part of India (not including one from the Governor-General, and six from his brother, Colonel Wellesley)—one hundred and twenty-four proposals for the hand of Miss Jowler! Cornet Gahagan," he continued, "I wish to think well of you: you are the bravest, the most modest, and, perhaps, the handsomest man in our corps; but you have not got a single rupee. You ask me for Julia, and you do not possess even an anna!"—(Here the old rogue grinned, as if he had made a capital pun.)—"No, no," said he, waxing good-natured; "Gagy my boy, it is nonsense! Julia love, retire with your mamma; this silly young gentleman will remain and smoke a pipe with me."

I took one: it was the bitterest chillum I ever smoked in my life.

I am not going to give here an account of my military services; they will appear in my great national autobiography, in forty volumes, which I am now preparing for the press. I was with my regiment in all Wellesley's brilliant campaigns; then taking dawk, I travelled across the country north-eastward, and had the honour of fighting by the side of Lord Lake at Laswaree, Degg, Furruckabad, Futtyghur, and Bhurtpore: but I will not boast of my actions—the military man knows them, MY SOVEREIGN appreciates them. If asked who was the bravest man of the Indian army, there is not an officer belonging to it who would not cry at once, GAHAGAN. The fact is, I was desperate: I cared not for life, deprived of Julia Jowler.

With Julia's stony looks ever before my eyes, her father's stern refusal in my ears, I did not care, at the close of the campaign, again to seek her company or to press my suit. We were eighteen months on service, marching and counter-marching, and fighting almost every other day: to the world I did not seem altered; but the world only saw the face, and not the seared and blighted heart within me. My valour, always desperate, now reached to a pitch of cruelty; I tortured my grooms and grass-cutters for the most trifling offence or error,—I never in action spared a man,—I sheared off three hundred and nine heads in the course of that single campaign.

Some influence, equally melancholy, seemed to have fallen upon poor old Jowler. About six months after we had left Dum Dum, he received a parcel of letters from Benares (whither his wife had retired with her daughter), and so deeply did they seem to weigh upon his spirits, that he ordered eleven men of his regiment to be flogged within two days; but it was against the blacks that he chiefly turned his wrath. Our fellows, in the heat and hurry of the campaign, were in the habit of dealing rather roughly with their prisoners, to extract treasure from them: they used to pull their nails out by the root, to boil them in kedgeree pots, to flog them and dress their wounds with cayenne pepper, and so on. Jowler, when he heard of these proceedings, which before had always justly exasperated him (he was a humane and kind little man), used now to smile fiercely and say, "D- the black scoundrels! Serve them right, serve them right!"

One day, about a couple of miles in advance of the column, I had been on a foraging-party with a few dragoons, and was returning peaceably to camp, when of a sudden a troop of Mahrattas burst on us from a neighbouring mango-tope, in which they had been hidden: in an instant three of my men's saddles were empty, and I was left with but seven more to make head against at least thirty of these vagabond black horsemen. I never saw in my life a nobler figure than the leader of the troop—mounted on a splendid black Arab; he was as tall, very nearly, as myself; he wore a steel cap and a shirt of mail, and carried a beautiful French carbine, which had already done execution upon two of my men. I saw that our only chance of safety lay in the destruction of this man. I shouted to him in a voice of thunder (in the Hindustanee tongue of course), "Stop, dog, if you dare, and encounter a man!"

In reply his lance came whirling in the air over my head, and mortally transfixed poor Foggarty of ours, who was behind me. Grinding my teeth and swearing horribly, I drew that scimitar which never yet failed its blow, and rushed at the Indian. He came down at full gallop, his own sword making ten thousand gleaming circles in the air, shrieking his cry of battle.

The contest did not last an instant. With my first blow I cut off his sword-arm at the wrist; my second I levelled at his head. I said that he wore a steel cap, with a gilt iron spike of six inches, and a hood of chain mail. I rose in my stirrups and delivered "St. George;" my sword caught the spike exactly on the point, split it sheer in two, cut crashing through the steel cap and hood, and was only stopped by a ruby which he wore in his back- plate. His head, cut clean in two between the eyebrows and nostrils, even between the two front teeth, fell one side on each shoulder, and he galloped on till his horse was stopped by my men, who were not a little amused at the feat.

As I had expected, the remaining ruffians fled on seeing their leader's fate. I took home his helmet by way of curiosity, and we made a single prisoner, who was instantly carried before old Jowler.

We asked the prisoner the name of the leader of the troop: he said it was Chowder Loll.

"Chowder Loll!" shrieked Colonel Jowler. "O Fate! thy hand is here!" He rushed wildly into his tent—the next day applied for leave of absence. Gutch took the command of the regiment, and I saw him no more for some time.

As I had distinguished myself not a little during the war, General Lake sent me up with despatches to Calcutta, where Lord Wellesley received me with the greatest distinction. Fancy my surprise, on going to a ball at Government House, to meet my old friend Jowler; my trembling, blushing, thrilling delight, when I saw Julia by his side!

Jowler seemed to blush too when he beheld me. I thought of my former passages with his daughter. "Gagy my boy," says he, shaking hands, "glad to see you. Old friend, Julia—come to tiffin— Hodgson's pale—brave fellow Gagy." Julia did not speak, but she turned ashy pale, and fixed upon me her awful eyes! I fainted almost, and uttered some incoherent words. Julia took my hand, gazed at me still, and said, "Come!" Need I say I went?

I will not go over the pale ale and currie-bhaut again! but this I know, that in half-an-hour I was as much in love as I ever had been: and that in three weeks I—yes, I—was the accepted lover of Julia! I did not pause to ask where were the one hundred and twenty-four offers? why I, refused before, should be accepted now? I only felt that I loved her, and was happy!

One night, one memorable night, I could not sleep, and, with a lover's pardonable passion, wandered solitary through the City of Palaces until I came to the house which contained my Julia. I peeped into the compound—all was still; I looked into the verandah—all was dark, except a light—yes, one light—and it was in Julia's chamber! My heart throbbed almost to stifling. I would—I WOULD advance, if but to gaze upon her for a moment, and to bless her as she slept. I DID look, I DID advance; and, O Heaven! I saw a lamp burning, Mrs. Jow. in a night-dress, with a very dark baby in her arms, and Julia looking tenderly at an ayah, who was nursing another.

"Oh, Mamma," said Julia, "what would that fool Gahagan say if he knew all?"

"HE DOES KNOW ALL!" shouted I, springing forward, and tearing down the tatties from the window. Mrs. Jow. ran shrieking out of the room, Julia fainted, the cursed black children squalled, and their d-d nurse fell on her knees, gabbling some infernal jargon of Hindustanee. Old Jowler at this juncture entered with a candle and a drawn sword.

"Liar! scoundrel! deceiver!" shouted I. "Turn, ruffian, and defend yourself!" But old Jowler, when he saw me, only whistled, looked at his lifeless daughter, and slowly left the room.

Why continue the tale? I need not now account for Jowler's gloom on receiving his letters from Benares—for his exclamation upon the death of the Indian chief—for his desire to marry his daughter: the woman I was wooing was no longer Miss Julia Jowler, she was Mrs. Chowder Loll!

CHAPTER II

ALLYGHUR AND LASWAREE

I sat down to write gravely and sadly, for (since the appearance of some of my adventures in a monthly magazine) unprincipled men have endeavoured to rob me of the only good I possess, to question the statements that I make, and, themselves without a spark of honour or good feeling, to steal from me that which is my sole wealth—my character as a teller of THE TRUTH.

The reader will understand that it is to the illiberal strictures of a profligate press I now allude; among the London journalists, none (luckily for themselves) have dared to question the veracity of my statements: they know me, and they know that I am IN LONDON. If I can use the pen, I can also wield a more manly and terrible weapon, and would answer their contradictions with my sword! No gold or gems adorn the hilt of that war-worn scimitar; but there is blood upon the blade—the blood of the enemies of my country, and the maligners of my honest fame. There are others, however—the disgrace of a disgraceful trade—who, borrowing from distance a despicable courage, have ventured to assail me. The infamous editors of the Kelso Champion, the Bungay Beacon, the Tipperary Argus, and the Stoke Pogis Sentinel, and other dastardly organs of the provincial press, have, although differing in politics, agreed upon this one point, and, with a scoundrelly unanimity, vented a flood of abuse upon the revelations made by me.

They say that I have assailed private characters, and wilfully perverted history to blacken the reputation of public men. I ask, was any one of these men in Bengal in the year 1803? Was any single conductor of any one of these paltry prints ever in Bundelcund or the Rohilla country? Does this EXQUISITE Tipperary scribe know the difference between Hurrygurrybang and Burrumtollah? Not he! and because, forsooth, in those strange and distant lands strange circumstances have taken place, it is insinuated that the relater is a liar: nay, that the very places themselves have no existence but in my imagination. Fools!—but I will not waste my anger upon them, and proceed to recount some other portions of my personal history.

It is, I presume, a fact which even THESE scribbling assassins will not venture to deny, that before the commencement of the campaign against Scindiah, the English General formed a camp at Kanouge on the Jumna, where he exercised that brilliant little army which was speedily to perform such wonders in the Dooab. It will be as well to give a slight account of the causes of a war which was speedily to rage through some of the fairest portions of the Indian continent.

Shah Allum, the son of Shah Lollum, the descendant by the female line of Nadir Shah (that celebrated Toorkomaun adventurer, who had well-nigh hurled Bajazet and Selim the Second from the throne of Bagdad)—Shah Allum, I say, although nominally the Emperor of Delhi, was in reality the slave of the various warlike chieftains who lorded it by turns over the country and the sovereign, until conquered and slain by some more successful rebel. Chowder Loll Masolgee, Zubberdust Khan, Dowsunt Row Scindiah, and the celebrated Bobbachy Jung Bahawder, had held for a time complete mastery in Delhi. The second of these, a ruthless Afghan soldier, had abruptly entered the capital; nor was he ejected from it until he had seized upon the principal jewels, and likewise put out the eyes of the last of the unfortunate family of Afrasiab. Scindiah came to the rescue of the sightless Shah Allum, and though he destroyed his oppressor, only increased his slavery; holding him in as painful a bondage as he had suffered under the tyrannous Afghan.

As long as these heroes were battling among themselves, or as long rather as it appeared that they had any strength to fight a battle, the British Government, ever anxious to see its enemies by the ears, by no means interfered in the contest. But the French Revolution broke out, and a host of starving sans-culottes appeared among the various Indian States, seeking for military service, and inflaming the minds of the various native princes against the British East India Company. A number of these entered into Scindiah's ranks: one of them, Perron, was commander of his army; and though that chief was as yet quite engaged in his hereditary quarrel with Jeswunt Row Holkar, and never thought of an invasion of the British territory, the Company all of a sudden discovered that Shah Allum, his sovereign, was shamefully ill-used, and determined to re-establish the ancient splendour of his throne.

Of course it was sheer benevolence for poor Shah Allum that prompted our governors to take these kindly measures in his favour. I don't know how it happened that, at the end of the war, the poor Shah was not a whit better off than at the beginning; and that though Holkar was beaten, and Scindiah annihilated, Shah Allum was much such a puppet as before. Somehow, in the hurry and confusion of this struggle, the oyster remained with the British Government, who had so kindly offered to dress it for the Emperor, while His Majesty was obliged to be contented with the shell.

The force encamped at Kanouge bore the title of the Grand Army of the Ganges and the Jumna; it consisted of eleven regiments of cavalry and twelve battalions of infantry, and was commanded by General Lake in person.

Well, on the 1st of September we stormed Perron's camp at Allyghur; on the fourth we took that fortress by assault; and as my name was mentioned in general orders, I may as well quote the Commander-in- Chief's words regarding me—they will spare me the trouble of composing my own eulogium:-

"The Commander-in-Chief is proud thus publicly to declare his high sense of the gallantry of Lieutenant Gahagan, of the — Cavalry. In the storming of the fortress, although unprovided with a single ladder, and accompanied but by a few brave men, Lieutenant Gahagan succeeded in escalading the inner and fourteenth wall of the place. Fourteen ditches lined with sword-blades and poisoned chevaux-de- frise, fourteen walls bristling with innumerable artillery and as smooth as looking-glasses, were in turn triumphantly passed by that enterprising officer. His course was to be traced by the heaps of slaughtered enemies lying thick upon the platforms; and alas! by the corpses of most of the gallant men who followed him! When at length he effected his lodgment, and the dastardly enemy, who dared not to confront him with arms, let loose upon him the tigers and lions of Scindiah's menagerie, this meritorious officer destroyed, with his own hand, four of the largest and most ferocious animals, and the rest, awed by the indomitable majesty of BRITISH VALOUR, shrank back to their dens. Thomas Higgory, a private, and Runty Goss, havildar, were the only two who remained out of the nine hundred who followed Lieutenant Gahagan. Honour to them! Honour and tears for the brave men who perished on that awful day!"

I have copied this, word for word, from the Bengal Hurkaru of September 24, 1803: and anybody who has the slightest doubt as to the statement, may refer to the paper itself.

And here I must pause to give thanks to Fortune, which so marvellously preserved me, Sergeant-Major Higgory, and Runty Goss. Were I to say that any valour of ours had carried us unhurt through this tremendous combat, the reader would laugh me to scorn. No: though my narrative is extraordinary, it is nevertheless authentic: and never never would I sacrifice truth for the mere sake of effect. The fact is this:- the citadel of Allyghur is situated upon a rock, about a thousand feet above the level of the sea, and is surrounded by fourteen walls, as his Excellency was good enough to remark in his despatch. A man who would mount these without scaling-ladders, is an ass; he who would SAY he mounted them without such assistance, is a liar and a knave. We HAD scaling- ladders at the commencement of the assault, although it was quite impossible to carry them beyond the first line of batteries. Mounted on them, however, as our troops were falling thick about me, I saw that we must ignominiously retreat, unless some other help could be found for our brave fellows to escalade the next wall. It was about seventy feet high. I instantly turned the guns of wall A on wall B, and peppered the latter so as to make, not a breach, but a scaling place; the men mounting in the holes made by the shot. By this simple stratagem, I managed to pass each successive barrier—for to ascend a wall which the General was pleased to call "as smooth as glass" is an absurd impossibility: I seek to achieve none such:-

"I dare do all that may become a man; Who dares do more, is neither more nor less."

Of course, had the enemy's guns been commonly well served, not one of us would ever have been alive out of the three; but whether it was owing to fright, or to the excessive smoke caused by so many pieces of artillery, arrive we did. On the platforms, too, our work was not quite so difficult as might be imagined—killing these fellows was sheer butchery. As soon as we appeared, they all turned and fled helter-skelter, and the reader may judge of their courage by the fact that out of about seven hundred men killed by us, only forty had wounds in front, the rest being bayoneted as they ran.

And beyond all other pieces of good fortune was the very letting out of these tigers; which was the dernier ressort of Bournonville, the second commandant of the fort. I had observed this man (conspicuous for a tricoloured scarf which he wore) upon every one of the walls as we stormed them, and running away the very first among the fugitives. He had all the keys of the gates; and in his tremor, as he opened the menagerie portal, left the whole bunch in the door, which I seized when the animals were overcome. Runty Goss then opened them one by one, our troops entered, and the victorious standard of my country floated on the walls of Allyghur!

When the General, accompanied by his staff, entered the last line of fortifications, the brave old man raised me from the dead rhinoceros on which I was seated, and pressed me to his breast. But the excitement which had borne me through the fatigues and perils of that fearful day failed all of a sudden, and I wept like a child upon his shoulder.

Promotion, in our army, goes unluckily by seniority; nor is it in the power of the General-in-Chief to advance a Caesar, if he finds him in the capacity of a subaltern: MY reward for the above exploit was, therefore, not very rich. His Excellency had a favourite horn snuff-box (for, though exalted in station, he was in his habits most simple): of this, and about a quarter of an ounce of high-dried Welsh, which he always took, he made me a present, saying, in front of the line, "Accept this, Mr. Gahagan, as a token of respect from the first to the bravest officer in the army."

Calculating the snuff to be worth a halfpenny, I should say that fourpence was about the value of this gift: but it has at least this good effect—it serves to convince any person who doubts my story, that the facts of it are really true. I have left it at the office of my publisher, along with the extract from the Bengal Hurkaru, and anybody may examine both by applying in the counting- house of Mr. Cunningham. That once popular expression, or proverb, "Are you up to snuff?" arose out of the above circumstance; for the officers of my corps, none of whom, except myself, had ventured on the storming party, used to twit me about this modest reward for my labours. Never mind! when they want me to storm a fort AGAIN, I shall know better.

Well, immediately after the capture of this important fortress, Perron, who had been the life and soul of Scindiah's army, came in to us, with his family and treasure, and was passed over to the French settlements at Chandernagur. Bourquien took his command, and against him we now moved. The morning of the 11th of September found us upon the plains of Delhi.

It was a burning hot day, and we were all refreshing ourselves after the morning's march, when I, who was on the advanced picket along with O'Gawler of the King's Dragoons, was made aware of the enemy's neighbourhood in a very singular manner. O'Gawler and I were seated under a little canopy of horse-cloths, which we had formed to shelter us from the intolerable heat of the sun, and were discussing with great delight a few Manilla cheroots, and a stone jar of the most exquisite, cool, weak, refreshing sangaree. We had been playing cards the night before, and O'Gawler had lost to me seven hundred rupees. I emptied the last of the sangaree into the two pint tumblers out of which we were drinking, and holding mine up, said, "Here's better luck to you next time, O'Gawler!"

As I spoke the words—whish!—a cannon-ball cut the tumbler clean out of my hand, and plumped into poor O'Gawler's stomach. It settled him completely, and of course I never got my seven hundred rupees. Such are the uncertainties of war!

To strap on my sabre and my accoutrements—to mount my Arab charger—to drink off what O'Gawler had left of the sangaree—and to gallop to the General, was the work of a moment. I found him as comfortably at tiffin as if he were at his own house in London.

"General," said I, as soon as I got into his paijamahs (or tent), "you must leave your lunch if you want to fight the enemy."

"The enemy—psha! Mr. Gahagan, the enemy is on the other side of the river."

"I can only tell your Excellency that the enemy's guns will hardly carry five miles, and that Cornet O'Gawler was this moment shot dead at my side with a cannon-ball."

"Ha! is it so?" said his Excellency, rising, and laying down the drumstick of a grilled chicken. "Gentlemen, remember that the eyes of Europe are upon us, and follow me!"

Each aide-de-camp started from table and seized his cocked hat; each British heart beat high at the thoughts of the coming melee. We mounted our horses, and galloped swiftly after the brave old General; I not the last in the train, upon my famous black charger.

It was perfectly true, the enemy were posted in force within three miles of our camp, and from a hillock in the advance to which we galloped, we were enabled with our telescopes to see the whole of his imposing line. Nothing can better describe it than this:-

_____ A /.................... /. /.

- A is the enemy, and the dots represent the hundred and twenty pieces of artillery which defended his line. He was moreover, entrenched; and a wide morass in his front gave him an additional security.

His Excellency for a moment surveyed the line, and then said, turning round to one of his aides-de-camp, "Order up Major-General Tinkler and the cavalry."

"HERE, does your Excellency mean?" said the aide-de-camp, surprised, for the enemy had perceived us, and the cannon-balls were flying about as thick as peas.

"HERE, SIR!" said the old General, stamping with his foot in a passion, and the A.D.C. shrugged his shoulders and galloped away. In five minutes we heard the trumpets in our camp, and in twenty more the greater part of the cavalry had joined us.

Up they came, five thousand men, their standards flapping in the air, their long line of polished jack-boots gleaming in the golden sunlight. "And now we are here," said Major-General Sir Theophilus Tinkler, "what next?" "Oh, d- it," said the Commander-in-Chief, "charge, charge—nothing like charging—galloping—guns—rascally black scoundrels—charge, charge!" And then turning round to me (perhaps he was glad to change the conversation), he said, "Lieutenant Gahagan, you will stay with me."

And well for him I did, for I do not hesitate to say that the battle WAS GAINED BY ME. I do not mean to insult the reader by pretending that any personal exertions of mine turned the day,— that I killed, for instance, a regiment of cavalry or swallowed a battery of guns,—such absurd tales would disgrace both the hearer and the teller. I, as is well known, never say a single word which cannot be proved, and hate more than all other vices the absurd sin of egotism: I simply mean that my ADVICE to the General, at a quarter-past two o'clock in the afternoon of that day, won this great triumph for the British army.

Gleig, Mill, and Thorn have all told the tale of this war, though somehow they have omitted all mention of the hero of it. General Lake, for the victory of that day, became Lord Lake of Laswaree. Laswaree! and who, forsooth, was the real conqueror of Laswaree? I can lay my hand upon my heart and say that I was. If any proof is wanting of the fact, let me give it at once, and from the highest military testimony in the world—I mean that of the Emperor Napoleon.

In the month of March, 1817, I was passenger on board the "Prince Regent," Captain Harris, which touched at St. Helena on its passage from Calcutta to England. In company with the other officers on board the ship, I paid my respects to the illustrious exile of Longwood, who received us in his garden, where he was walking about, in a nankeen dress and a large broad-brimmed straw hat, with General Montholon, Count Las Casas, and his son Emanuel, then a little boy; who I dare say does not recollect me, but who nevertheless played with my sword-knot and the tassels of my Hessian boots during the whole of our interview with his Imperial Majesty.

Our names were read out (in a pretty accent, by the way!) by General Montholon, and the Emperor, as each was pronounced, made a bow to the owner of it, but did not vouchsafe a word. At last Montholon came to mine. The Emperor looked me at once in the face, took his hands out of his pockets, put them behind his back, and coming up to me smiling, pronounced the following words:-

"Assaye, Delhi, Deeg, Futtyghur?"

I blushed, and, taking off my hat with a bow, said, "Sire, c'est moi."

"Parbleu! je le savais bien," said the Emperor, holding out his snuff-box. "En usez-vous, Major?" I took a large pinch (which, with the honour of speaking to so great a man, brought the tears into my eyes), and he continued as nearly as possible in the following words:-

"Sir, you are known; you come of an heroic nation. Your third brother, the Chef de Bataillon, Count Godfrey Gahagan, was in my Irish Brigade."

Gahagan. "Sire, it is true. He and my countrymen in your Majesty's service stood under the green flag in the breach of Burgos, and beat Wellington back. It was the only time, as your Majesty knows, that Irishmen and Englishmen were beaten in that war."

Napoleon (looking as if he would say, "D- your candour, Major Gahagan"). "Well, well; it was so. Your brother was a Count, and died a General in my service."

Gahagan. "He was found lying upon the bodies of nine-and-twenty Cossacks at Borodino. They were all dead, and bore the Gahagan mark."

Napoleon (to Montholon). "C'est vrai, Montholon: je vous donne ma parole d'honneur la plus sacree, que c'est vrai. Ils ne sont pas d'autres, ces terribles Ga'gans. You must know that Monsieur gained the battle of Delhi as certainly as I did that of Austerlitz. In this way:- Ce belitre de Lor Lake, after calling up his cavalry, and placing them in front of Holkar's batteries, qui balayaient la plaine, was for charging the enemy's batteries with his horse, who would have been ecrases, mitrailles, foudroyes to a man but for the cunning of ce grand rogue que vous voyez."

Montholon. "Coquin de Major, va!"

Napoleon. "Montholon! tais-toi. When Lord Lake, with his great bull-headed English obstinacy, saw the facheuse position into which he had brought his troops, he was for dying on the spot, and would infallibly have done so—and the loss of his army would have been the ruin of the East India Company— and the ruin of the English East India Company would have established my Empire (bah! it was a republic then!) in the East—but that the man before us, Lieutenant Goliah Gahagan, was riding at the side of General Lake."

Montholon (with an accent of despair and fury). "Gredin! cent mille tonnerres de Dieu!"

Napoleon (benignantly). "Calme-toi, mon fidele ami. What will you? It was fate. Gahagan, at the critical period of the battle, or rather slaughter (for the English had not slain a man of the enemy), advised a retreat."

Montholon. "Le lache! Un Francais meurt, mais il ne recule jamais."

Napoleon. "Stupide! Don't you see why the retreat was ordered?— don't you know that it was a feint on the part of Gahagan to draw Holkar from his impregnable entrenchments? Don't you know that the ignorant Indian fell into the snare, and issuing from behind the cover of his guns, came down with his cavalry on the plains in pursuit of Lake and his dragoons? Then it was that the Englishmen turned upon him; the hardy children of the North swept down his feeble horsemen, bore them back to their guns, which were useless, entered Holkar's entrenchments along with his troops, sabred the artillerymen at their pieces, and won the battle of Delhi!"

As the Emperor spoke, his pale cheek glowed red, his eye flashed fire, his deep clear voice rung as of old when he pointed out the enemy from beneath the shadow of the Pyramids, or rallied his regiments to the charge upon the death-strewn plain of Wagram. I have had many a proud moment in my life, but never such a proud one as this; and I would readily pardon the word "coward," as applied to me by Montholon, in consideration of the testimony which his master bore in my favour.

"Major," said the Emperor to me in conclusion, "why had I not such a man as you in my service? I would have made you a Prince and a Marshal!" and here he fell into a reverie, of which I knew and respected the purport. He was thinking, doubtless, that I might have retrieved his fortunes; and indeed I have very little doubt that I might.

Very soon after, coffee was brought by Monsieur Marchand, Napoleon's valet-de-chambre, and after partaking of that beverage, and talking upon the politics of the day, the Emperor withdrew, leaving me deeply impressed by the condescension he had shown in this remarkable interview.

CHAPTER III

A PEEP INTO SPAIN—ACCOUNT OF THE ORIGIN AND SERVICES OF THE AHMEDNUGGAR IRREGULARS

HEADQUARTERS, MORELLA: September 15, 1838

I have been here for some months, along with my young friend Cabrera: and in the hurry and bustle of war—daily on guard and in the batteries for sixteen hours out of the twenty-four, with fourteen severe wounds and seven musket-balls in my body—it may be imagined that I have had little time to think about the publication of my memoirs. Inter arma silent leges—in the midst of fighting be hanged to writing! as the poet says; and I never would have bothered myself with a pen, had not common gratitude incited me to throw off a few pages.

Along with Oraa's troops, who have of late been beleaguering this place, there was a young Milesian gentleman, Mr. Toone O'Connor Emmett Fitzgerald Sheeny by name, a law student, and a member of Gray's Inn, and what he called Bay Ah of Trinity College, Dublin. Mr. Sheeny was with the Queen's people, not in a military capacity, but as representative of an English journal; to which, for a trifling weekly remuneration, he was in the habit of transmitting accounts of the movements of the belligerents, and his own opinion of the politics of Spain. Receiving, for the discharge of his duty, a couple of guineas a week from the proprietors of the journal in question, he was enabled, as I need scarcely say, to make such a show in Oraa's camp as only a Christino general officer, or at the very least a colonel of a regiment, can afford to keep up.

In the famous sortie which we made upon the twenty-third, I was of course among the foremost in the melee, and found myself, after a good deal of slaughtering (which it would be as disagreeable as useless to describe here), in the court of a small inn or podesta, which had been made the headquarters of several Queenite officers during the siege. The pesatero or landlord of the inn had been despatched by my brave chapel-churies, with his fine family of children—the officers quartered in the podesta had of course bolted; but one man remained, and my fellows were on the point of cutting him into ten thousand pieces with their borachios, when I arrived in the room time enough to prevent the catastrophe. Seeing before me an individual in the costume of a civilian—a white hat, a light blue satin cravat, embroidered with butterflies and other quadrupeds, a green coat and brass buttons, and a pair of blue plaid trousers, I recognised at once a countryman, and interposed to save his life.

In an agonised brogue the unhappy young man was saying all that he could to induce the chapel-churies to give up their intention of slaughtering him; but it is very little likely that his protestations would have had any effect upon them, had not I appeared in the room, and shouted to the ruffians to hold their hand.

Seeing a general officer before them (I have the honour to hold that rank in the service of His Catholic Majesty), and moreover one six feet four in height, and armed with that terrible cabecilla (a sword so called, because it is five feet long) which is so well known among the Spanish armies—seeing, I say, this figure, the fellows retired, exclaiming, "Adios, corpo di bacco nosotros," and so on, clearly proving (by their words) that they would, if they dared, have immolated the victim whom I had thus rescued from their fury. "Villains!" shouted I, hearing them grumble, "away! quit the apartment!" Each man, sulkily sheathing his sombrero, obeyed, and quitted the camarilla.

It was then that Mr. Sheeny detailed to me the particulars to which I have briefly adverted; and, informing me at the same time that he had a family in England who would feel obliged to me for his release, and that his most intimate friend the English Ambassador would move heaven and earth to revenge his fall, he directed my attention to a portmanteau passably well filled, which he hoped would satisfy the cupidity of my troops. I said, though with much regret, that I must subject his person to a search; and hence arose the circumstance which has called for what I fear you will consider a somewhat tedious explanation. I found upon Mr. Sheeny's person three sovereigns in English money (which I have to this day), and singularly enough a copy of the New Monthly Magazine, containing a portion of my adventures. It was a toss-up whether I should let the poor young man be shot or no, but this little circumstance saved his life. The gratified vanity of authorship induced me to accept his portmanteau and valuables, and to allow the poor wretch to go free. I put the Magazine in my coat-pocket, and left him and the podesta.

The men, to my surprise, had quitted the building, and it was full time for me to follow; for I found our sallying party, after committing dreadful ravages in Oraa's lines, were in full retreat upon the fort, hotly pressed by a superior force of the enemy. I am pretty well known and respected by the men of both parties in Spain (indeed I served for some months on the Queen's side before I came over to Don Carlos); and, as it is my maxim never to give quarter, I never expect to receive it when taken myself. On issuing from the podesta with Sheeny's portmanteau and my sword in my hand, I was a little disgusted and annoyed to see our own men in a pretty good column retreating at double-quick, and about four hundred yards beyond me, up the hill leading to the fort; while on my left hand, and at only a hundred yards, a troop of the Queenite lancers were clattering along the road.

I had got into the very middle of the road before I made this discovery, so that the fellows had a full sight of me, and whizz! came a bullet by my left whisker before I could say Jack Robinson. I looked round—there were seventy of the accursed malvados at the least, and within, as I said, a hundred yards. Were I to say that I stopped to fight seventy men, you would write me down a fool or a liar: no, sir, I did not fight, I ran away.

I am six feet four—my figure is as well known in the Spanish army as that of the Count de Luchana, or my fierce little friend Cabrera himself. "GAHAGAN!" shouted out half-a-dozen scoundrelly voices, and fifty more shots came rattling after me. I was running— running as the brave stag before the hounds— running as I have done a great number of times before in my life, when there was no help for it but a race.

After I had run about five hundred yards, I saw that I had gained nearly three upon our column in front, and that likewise the Christino horsemen were left behind some hundred yards more; with the exception of three, who were fearfully near me. The first was an officer without a lance; he had fired both his pistols at me, and was twenty yards in advance of his comrades; there was a similar distance between the two lancers who rode behind him. I determined then to wait for No. 1, and as he came up delivered cut 3 at his horse's near leg—off it flew, and down, as I expected, went horse and man. I had hardly time to pass my sword through my prostrate enemy, when No. 2 was upon me. If I could but get that fellow's horse, thought I, I am safe; and I executed at once the plan which I hoped was to effect my rescue.

I had, as I said, left the podesta with Sheeny's portmanteau, and, unwilling to part with some of the articles it contained—some shirts, a bottle of whisky, a few cakes of Windsor soap, &c. &c.,— I had carried it thus far on my shoulders, but now was compelled to sacrifice it malgre moi. As the lancer came up, I dropped my sword from my right hand, and hurled the portmanteau at his head, with aim so true, that he fell back on his saddle like a sack, and thus when the horse galloped up to me, I had no difficulty in dismounting the rider: the whisky-bottle struck him over his right eye, and he was completely stunned. To dash him from the saddle and spring myself into it, was the work of a moment; indeed, the two combats had taken place in about a fifth part of the time which it has taken the reader to peruse the description. But in the rapidity of the last encounter, and the mounting of my enemy's horse, I had committed a very absurd oversight—I was scampering away WITHOUT MY SWORD! What was I to do?— to scamper on, to be sure, and trust to the legs of my horse for safety!

The lancer behind me gained on me every moment, and I could hear his horrid laugh as he neared me. I leaned forward jockey-fashion in my saddle, and kicked, and urged, and flogged with my hand, but all in vain. Closer—closer—the point of his lance was within two feet of my back. Ah! ah! he delivered the point, and fancy my agony when I felt it enter—through exactly fifty-nine pages of the New Monthly Magazine. Had it not been for that Magazine, I should have been impaled without a shadow of a doubt. Was I wrong in feeling gratitude? Had I not cause to continue my contributions to that periodical?

When I got safe into Morella, along with the tail of the sallying party, I was for the first time made acquainted with the ridiculous result of the lancer's thrust (as he delivered his lance, I must tell you that a ball came whizz over my head from our fellows, and entering at his nose, put a stop to his lancing for the future). I hastened to Cabrera's quarter, and related to him some of my adventures during the day.

"But, General," said he, "you are standing. I beg you chiudete l'uscio (take a chair)."

I did so, and then for the first time was aware that there was some foreign substance in the tail of my coat, which prevented my sitting at ease. I drew out the Magazine which I had seized, and there, to my wonder, discovered the Christino lance twisted up like a fish-hook or a pastoral crook.

"Ha! ha! ha!" said Cabrera (who is a notorious wag).

"Valdepenas madrilenos," growled out Tristany.

"By my cachuca di caballero (upon my honour as a gentleman)," shrieked out Ros d'Eroles, convulsed with laughter, "I will send it to the Bishop of Leon for a crozier."

"Gahagan has CONSECRATED it," giggled out Ramon Cabrera; and so they went on with their muchacas for an hour or more. But, when they heard that the means of my salvation from the lance of the scoundrelly Christino had been the Magazine containing my own history, their laugh was changed into wonder. I read them (speaking Spanish more fluently than English) every word of my story. "But how is this?" said Cabrera. "You surely have other adventures to relate?"

"Excellent sir," said I, "I have;" and that very evening, as we sat over our cups of tertullia (sangaree), I continued my narrative in nearly the following words:-

"I left off in the very middle of the battle of Delhi, which ended, as everybody knows, in the complete triumph of the British arms. But who gained the battle? Lord Lake is called Viscount Lake of Delhi and Laswaree, while Major Gaha—nonsense, never mind HIM, never mind the charge he executed when, sabre in hand, he leaped the six-foot wall in the mouth of the roaring cannon, over the heads of the gleaming pikes; when, with one hand seizing the sacred peishcush, or fish—which was the banner always borne before Scindiah,—he, with his good sword, cut off the trunk of the famous white elephant, which, shrieking with agony, plunged madly into the Mahratta ranks, followed by his giant brethren, tossing, like chaff before the wind, the affrighted kitmatgars. He, meanwhile, now plunging into the midst of a battalion of consomahs, now cleaving to the chine a screaming and ferocious bobbachee, rushed on, like the simoom across the red Zaharan plain, killing, with his own hand, a hundred and forty-thr—but never mind—'ALONE HE DID IT;' sufficient be it for him, however, that the victory was won: he cares not for the empty honours which were awarded to more fortunate men!

"We marched after the battle to Delhi, where poor blind old Shah Allum received us, and bestowed all kinds of honours and titles on our General. As each of the officers passed before him, the Shah did not fail to remark my person, and was told my name.

"Lord Lake whispered to him my exploits, and the old man was so delighted with the account of my victory over the elephant (whose trunk I use to this day), that he said, 'Let him be called GUJPUTI,' or the lord of elephants; and Gujputi was the name by which I was afterwards familiarly known among the natives,—the men, that is. The women had a softer appellation for me, and called me 'Mushook,' or charmer.

"Well, I shall not describe Delhi, which is doubtless well known to the reader; nor the siege of Agra, to which place we went from Delhi; nor the terrible day at Laswaree, which went nigh to finish the war.

Suffice it to say that we were victorious, and that I was wounded; as I have invariably been in the two hundred and four occasions when I have found myself in action. One point, however, became in the course of this campaign QUITE evident—THAT SOMETHING MUST BE DONE FOR GAHAGAN. The country cried shame, the King's troops grumbled, the sepoys openly murmured that their Gujputi was only a lieutenant, when he had performed such signal services. What was to be done? Lord Wellesley was in an evident quandary. 'Gahagan,' wrote he, 'to be a subaltern is evidently not your fate- -YOU WERE BORN FOR COMMAND; but Lake and General Wellesley are good officers, they cannot be turned out—I must make a post for you. What say you, my dear fellow, to a corps of IRREGULAR HORSE?'

"It was thus that the famous corps of AHMEDNUGGAR IRREGULARS had its origin; a guerilla force, it is true, but one which will long be remembered in the annals of our Indian campaigns.

"As the commander of this regiment, I was allowed to settle the uniform of the corps, as well as to select recruits. These were not wanting as soon as my appointment was made known, but came flocking to my standard a great deal faster than to the regular corps in the Company's service. I had European officers, of course, to command them, and a few of my countrymen as sergeants; the rest were all natives, whom I chose of the strongest and bravest men in India; chiefly Pitans, Afghans, Hurrumzadehs, and Calliawns: for these are well known to be the most warlike districts of our Indian territory.

"When on parade and in full uniform we made a singular and noble appearance. I was always fond of dress; and, in this instance gave a carte blanche to my taste, and invented the most splendid costume that ever perhaps decorated a soldier. I am, as I have stated already, six feet four inches in height, and of matchless symmetry and proportion. My hair and beard are of the most brilliant auburn, so bright as scarcely to be distinguished at a distance from scarlet. My eyes are bright blue, overshadowed by bushy eyebrows of the colour of my hair, and a terrific gash of the deepest purple, which goes over the forehead, the eyelid, and the cheek, and finishes at the ear, gives my face a more strictly military appearance than can be conceived. When I have been drinking (as is pretty often the case) this gash becomes ruby bright, and as I have another which took off a piece of my under- lip, and shows five of my front teeth, I leave you to imagine that 'seldom lighted on the earth' (as the monster Burke remarked of one of his unhappy victims) 'a more extraordinary vision.' I improved these natural advantages; and, while in cantonment during the hot winds at Chittybobbary, allowed my hair to grow very long, as did my beard, which reached to my waist. It took me two hours daily to curl my hair in ten thousand little corkscrew ringlets, which waved over my shoulders, and to get my moustaches well round to the corners of my eyelids. I dressed in loose scarlet trousers and red morocco boots, a scarlet jacket, and a shawl of the same colour round my waist; a scarlet turban three feet high, and decorated with a tuft of the scarlet feathers of the flamingo, formed my head-dress, and I did not allow myself a single ornament, except a small silver skull and cross-bones in front of my turban. Two brace of pistols, a Malay creese, and a tulwar, sharp on both sides, and very nearly six feet in length, completed this elegant costume. My two flags were each surmounted with a real skull and cross-bones, and ornamented one with a black, and the other with a red beard (of enormous length, taken from men slain in battle by me). On one flag were of course the arms of John Company; on the other, an image of myself bestriding a prostrate elephant, with the simple word 'GUJPUTI' written underneath in the Nagaree, Persian, and Sanscrit characters. I rode my black horse, and looked, by the immortal gods, like Mars. To me might be applied the words which were written concerning handsome General Webb, in Marlborough's time:-

"'To noble danger he conducts the way, His great example all his troop obey, Before the front the Major sternly rides, With such an air as Mars to battle strides. Propitious Heaven must sure a hero save Like Paris handsome, and like Hector brave!'

"My officers (Captains Biggs and Mackanulty, Lieutenants Glogger, Pappendick, Stuffle, &c. &c.) were dressed exactly in the same way, but in yellow; and the men were similarly equipped, but in black. I have seen many regiments since, and many ferocious-looking men, but the Ahmednuggar Irregulars were more dreadful to the view than any set of ruffians on which I ever set eyes. I would to Heaven that the Czar of Muscovy had passed through Cabool and Lahore, and that I with my old Ahmednuggars stood on a fair field to meet him! Bless you, bless you, my swart companions in victory! through the mist of twenty years I hear the booming of your war-cry, and mark the glitter of your scimitars as ye rage in the thickest of the battle!

"But away with melancholy reminiscences. You may fancy what a figure the Irregulars cut on a field-day—a line of five hundred black-faced, black-dressed, black-horsed, black-bearded men—Biggs, Glogger, and the other officers in yellow, galloping about the field like flashes of lightning; myself enlightening them, red, solitary, and majestic, like yon glorious orb in heaven.

"There are very few men, I presume, who have not heard of Holkar's sudden and gallant incursion into the Dooab, in the year 1804, when we thought that the victory of Laswaree and the brilliant success at Deeg had completely finished him. Taking ten thousand horse he broke up his camp at Palimbang; and the first thing General Lake heard of him was, that he was at Putna, then at Rumpooge, then at Doncaradam—he was, in fact, in the very heart of our territory.

"The unfortunate part of the affair was this:- His Excellency, despising the Mahratta chieftain, had allowed him to advance about two thousand miles in his front, and knew not in the slightest degree where to lay hold on him. Was he at Hazarubaug? was he at Bogly Gunge? nobody knew, and for a considerable period the movements of Lake's cavalry were quite ambiguous, uncertain, promiscuous, and undetermined.

"Such, briefly, was the state of affairs in October 1804. At the beginning of that month I had been wounded (a trifling scratch, cutting off my left upper eyelid, a bit of my cheek, and my under- lip), and I was obliged to leave Biggs in command of my Irregulars, whilst I retired for my wounds to an English station at Furruckabad, alias Futtyghur—it is, as every twopenny postman knows, at the apex of the Dooab. We have there a cantonment, and thither I went for the mere sake of the surgeon and the sticking- plaster.

"Furruckabad, then, is divided into two districts or towns: the lower Cotwal, inhabited by the natives, and the upper (which is fortified slightly, and has all along been called Futtyghur, meaning in Hindustanee 'the-favourite-resort-of-the-white-faced- Feringhees-near-the-mango-tope-consecrated-to-Ram'), occupied by Europeans. (It is astonishing, by the way, how comprehensive that language is, and how much can be conveyed in one or two of the commonest phrases.)

"Biggs, then, and my men were playing all sorts of wondrous pranks with Lord Lake's army, whilst I was detained an unwilling prisoner of health at Futtyghur.

"An unwilling prisoner, however, I should not say. The cantonment at Futtyghur contained that which would have made any man a happy slave. Woman, lovely woman, was there in abundance and variety!

The fact is, that, when the campaign commenced in 1803, the ladies of the army all congregated to this place, where they were left, as it was supposed, in safety. I might, like Homer, relate the names and qualities of all. I may at least mention SOME whose memory is still most dear to me. There was -

"Mrs. Major-General Bulcher, wife of Bulcher of the Infantry.

"Miss Bulcher.

"MISS BELINDA BULCHER (whose name I beg the printer to place in large capitals).

"Mrs. Colonel Vandegobbleschroy.

"Mrs. Major Macan and the four Misses Macan.

"The Honourable Mrs. Burgoo, Mrs. Flix, Hicks, Wicks, and many more too numerous to mention. The flower of our camp was, however, collected there, and the last words of Lord Lake to me, as I left him, were, 'Gahagan, I commit those women to your charge. Guard them with your life, watch over them with your honour, defend them with the matchless power of your indomitable arm.'

"Futtyghur is, as I have said, a European station, and the pretty air of the bungalows, amid the clustering topes of mango-trees, has often ere this excited the admiration of the tourist and sketcher. On the brow of a hill—the Burrumpooter river rolls majestically at its base; and no spot, in a word, can be conceived more exquisitely arranged, both by art and nature, as a favourite residence of the British fair. Mrs. Bulcher, Mrs. Vandegobbleschroy, and the other married ladies above mentioned, had each of them delightful bungalows and gardens in the place, and between one cottage and another my time passed as delightfully as can the hours of any man who is away from his darling occupation of war.

"I was the commandant of the fort. It is a little insignificant pettah, defended simply by a couple of gabions, a very ordinary counterscarp, and a bomb-proof embrasure. On the top of this my flag was planted, and the small garrison of forty men only were comfortably barracked off in the casemates within. A surgeon and two chaplains (there were besides three reverend gentlemen of amateur missions, who lived in the town), completed, as I may say, the garrison of our little fortalice, which I was left to defend and to command.

"On the night of the first of November, in the year 1804, I had invited Mrs. Major-General Bulcher and her daughters, Mrs. Vandegobbleschroy, and, indeed, all the ladies in the cantonment, to a little festival in honour of the recovery of my health, of the commencement of the shooting season, and indeed as a farewell visit, for it was my intention to take dawk the very next morning and return to my regiment. The three amateur missionaries whom I have mentioned, and some ladies in the cantonment of very rigid religious principles, refused to appear at my little party. They had better never have been born than have done as they did: as you shall hear.

"We had been dancing merrily all night, and the supper (chiefly of the delicate condor, the luscious adjutant, and other birds of a similar kind, which I had shot in the course of the day) had been duly feted by every lady and gentleman present; when I took an opportunity to retire on the ramparts, with the interesting and lovely Belinda Bulcher. I was occupied, as the French say, in CONTER-ing fleurettes to this sweet young creature, when, all of a sudden, a rocket was seen whizzing through the air, and a strong light was visible in the valley below the little fort.

"'What, fireworks! Captain Gahagan,' said Belinda; 'this is too gallant.'

"'Indeed, my dear Miss Bulcher,' said I, 'they are fireworks of which I have no idea: perhaps our friends the missionaries—'

"'Look, look!' said Belinda, trembling, and clutching tightly hold of my arm: 'what do I see? yes—no—yes! it is—OUR BUNGALOW IS IN FLAMES!'

"It was true, the spacious bungalow occupied by Mrs. Major-General was at that moment seen a prey to the devouring element—another and another succeeded it—seven bungalows, before I could almost ejaculate the name of Jack Robinson, were seen blazing brightly in the black midnight air!

"I seized my night-glass, and looking towards the spot where the conflagration raged, what was my astonishment to see thousands of black forms dancing round the fires; whilst by their lights I could observe columns after columns of Indian horse, arriving and taking up their ground in the very middle of the open square or tank, round which the bungalows were built!

"'Ho, warder!' shouted I (while the frightened and trembling Belinda clung closer to my side, and pressed the stalwart arm that encircled her waist), 'down with the drawbridge! see that your masolgees' (small tumbrels which are used in place of large artillery) 'be well loaded: you, sepoys, hasten and man the ravelin! you, choprasees, put out the lights in the embrasures! we shall have warm work of it to-night, or my name is not Goliah Gahagan.'

"The ladies, the guests (to the number of eighty-three), the sepoys, choprasees, masolgees, and so on, had all crowded on the platform at the sound of my shouting, and dreadful was the consternation, shrill the screaming, occasioned by my words. The men stood irresolute and mute with terror; the women, trembling, knew scarcely whither to fly for refuge. 'Who are yonder ruffians?' said I. A hundred voices yelped in reply—some said the Pindarees, some said the Mahrattas, some vowed it was Scindiah, and others declared it was Holkar—no one knew.

"'Is there any one here,' said I, 'who will venture to reconnoitre yonder troops?' There was a dead pause.

"'A thousand tomauns to the man who will bring me news of yonder army!' again I repeated. Still a dead silence. The fact was that Scindiah and Holkar both were so notorious for their cruelty, that no one dared venture to face the danger. 'Oh for fifty of my brave Ahmednuggarees!' thought I.

"'Gentlemen,' said I, 'I see it—you are cowards—none of you dare encounter the chance even of death. It is an encouraging prospect: know you not that the ruffian Holkar, if it be he, will with to- morrow's dawn beleaguer our little fort, and throw thousands of men against our walls? know you not that, if we are taken, there is no quarter, no hope; death for us—and worse than death for these lovely ones assembled here?' Here the ladies shrieked and raised a howl as I have heard the jackals on a summer's evening. Belinda, my dear Belinda! flung both her arms round me, and sobbed on my shoulder (or in my waistcoat-pocket rather, for the little witch could reach no higher).

"'Captain Gahagan,' sobbed she, 'Go-Go-Goggle-iah!'

"'My soul's adored!' replied I.

"'Swear to me one thing.'

"'I swear.'

"'That if—that if—the nasty, horrid, odious black Mah-ra-a-a- attahs take the fort, you will put me out of their power.'

"I clasped the dear girl to my heart, and swore upon my sword that, rather than she should incur the risk of dishonour, she should perish by my own hand. This comforted her; and her mother, Mrs. Major-General Bulcher, and her elder sister, who had not until now known a word of our attachment, (indeed, but for these extraordinary circumstances, it is probable that we ourselves should never have discovered it), were under these painful circumstances made aware of my beloved Belinda's partiality for me. Having communicated thus her wish of self-destruction, I thought her example a touching and excellent one, and proposed to all the ladies that they should follow it, and that at the entry of the enemy into the fort, and at a signal given by me, they should one and all make away with themselves. Fancy my disgust when, after making this proposition, not one of the ladies chose to accede to it, and received it with the same chilling denial that my former proposal to the garrison had met with.

"In the midst of this hurry and confusion, as if purposely to add to it, a trumpet was heard at the gate of the fort, and one of the sentinels came running to me, saying that a Mahratta soldier was before the gate with a flag of truce!

"I went down, rightly conjecturing, as it turned out, that the party, whoever they might be, had no artillery; and received at the point of my sword a scroll of which the following is a translation.

"'To Goliah Gahagan Gujputi.

"'LORD OF ELEPHANTS, SIR,—I have the honour to inform you that I arrived before this place at eight o'clock p.m. with ten thousand cavalry under my orders. I have burned, since my arrival, seventeen bungalows in Furruckabad and Futtyghur, and have likewise been under the painful necessity of putting to death three clergymen (mollahs) and seven English officers, whom I found in the village; the women have been transferred to safe keeping in the harems of my officers and myself.

"'As I know your courage and talents, I shall be very happy if you will surrender the fortress, and take service as a major-general (hookahbadar) in my army. Should my proposal not meet with your assent, I beg leave to state that to-morrow I shall storm the fort, and on taking it, shall put to death every male in the garrison, and every female above twenty years of age. For yourself I shall reserve a punishment, which for novelty and exquisite torture has, I flatter myself, hardly ever been exceeded. Awaiting the favour of a reply, I am, Sir,

"'Your very obedient servant,

"'JESWUNT ROW HOLKAR. "'CAMP BEFORE FUTTYGHUR: September 1, 1804. "'R. S. V. P.'

"The officer who had brought this precious epistle (it is astonishing how Holkar had aped the forms of English correspondence), an enormous Pitan soldier, with a shirt of mail, and a steel cap and cape, round which his turban wound, was leaning against the gate on his matchlock, and whistling a national melody. I read the letter, and saw at once there was no time to be lost. That man, thought I, must never go back to Holkar. Were he to attack us now before we were prepared, the fort would be his in half-an-hour.

"Tying my white pocket-handkerchief to a stick, I flung open the gate and advanced to the officer: he was standing, I said, on the little bridge across the moat. I made him a low salaam, after the fashion of the country, and, as he bent forward to return the compliment, I am sorry to say, I plunged forward, gave him a violent blow on the head, which deprived him of all sensation, and then dragged him within the wall, raising the drawbridge after me.

"I bore the body into my own apartment; there, swift as thought, I stripped him of his turban, cammerbund, peijammahs, and papooshes, and, putting them on myself, determined to go forth and reconnoitre the enemy."

Here I was obliged to stop, for Cabrera, Ros d'Eroles, and the rest of the staff, were sound asleep! What I did in my reconnaissance, and how I defended the fort of Futtyghur, I shall have the honour of telling on another occasion.

CHAPTER IV

THE INDIAN CAMP—THE SORTIE FROM THE FORT

HEADQUARTERS, MORELLA: October 3, 1838

It is a balmy night. I hear the merry jingle of the tambourine, and the cheery voices of the girls and peasants, as they dance beneath my casement, under the shadow of the clustering vines. The laugh and song pass gaily round, and even at this distance I can distinguish the elegant form of Ramon Cabrera, as he whispers gay nothings in the ears of the Andalusian girls, or joins in the thrilling chorus of Riego's hymn, which is ever and anon vociferated by the enthusiastic soldiery of Carlos Quinto. I am alone, in the most inaccessible and most bomb-proof tower of our little fortalice; the large casements are open— the wind, as it enters, whispers in my ear its odorous recollections of the orange grove and the myrtle bower. My torch (a branch of the fragrant cedar-tree) flares and flickers in the midnight breeze, and disperses its scent and burning splinters on my scroll and the desk where I write—meet implements for a soldier's authorship!—it is CARTRIDGE paper over which my pen runs so glibly, and a yawning barrel of gunpowder forms my rough writing-table. Around me, below me, above me, all—all is peace! I think, as I sit here so lonely, on my country, England! and muse over the sweet and bitter recollections of my early days! Let me resume my narrative, at the point where (interrupted by the authoritative summons of war) I paused on the last occasion.

I left off, I think—(for I am a thousand miles away from proof-sheets as I write, and, were I not writing the simple TRUTH, must contradict myself a thousand times in the course of my tale)—I think, I say, that I left off at that period of my story, when, Holkar being before Futtyghur, and I in command of that fortress, I had just been compelled to make away with his messenger: and, dressed in the fallen Indian's accoutrements, went forth to reconnoitre the force, and, if possible, to learn the intentions of the enemy. However much my figure might have resembled that of the Pitan, and, disguised in his armour, might have deceived the lynx-eyed Mahrattas, into whose camp I was about to plunge, it was evident that a single glance at my fair face and auburn beard would have undeceived the dullest blockhead in Holkar's army. Seizing, then, a bottle of Burgess's walnut catsup, I dyed my face and my hands, and, with the simple aid of a flask of Warren's jet, I made my hair and beard as black as ebony. The Indian's helmet and chain hood covered likewise a great part of my face, and I hoped thus, with luck, impudence, and a complete command of all the Eastern dialects and languages, from Burmah to Afghanistan, to pass scot-free through this somewhat dangerous ordeal.

I had not the word of the night, it is true—but I trusted to good fortune for that, and passed boldly out of the fortress, bearing the flag of truce as before; I had scarcely passed on a couple of hundred yards, when lo! a party of Indian horsemen, armed like him I had just overcome, trotted towards me. One was leading a noble white charger, and no sooner did he see me than, dismounting from his own horse, and giving the rein to a companion, he advanced to meet me with the charger; a second fellow likewise dismounted and followed the first: one held the bridle of the horse, while the other (with a multitude of salaams, aleikums, and other genuflexions) held the jewelled stirrup, and kneeling, waited until I should mount.

I took the hint at once: the Indian who had come up to the fort was a great man—that was evident; I walked on with a majestic air, gathered up the velvet reins, and sprung into the magnificent high-peaked saddle. "Buk, buk," said I. "It is good. In the name of the forty-nine Imaums, let us ride on." And the whole party set off at a brisk trot, I keeping silence, and thinking with no little trepidation of what I was about to encounter.

As we rode along, I heard two of the men commenting upon my unusual silence (for I suppose, I—that is the Indian—was a talkative officer). "The lips of the Bahawder are closed," said one. "Where are those birds of Paradise, his long-tailed words? they are imprisoned between the golden bars of his teeth!"

"Kush," said his companion, "be quiet! Bobbachy Bahawder has seen the dreadful Feringhee, Gahagan Khan Gujputi, the elephant-lord, whose sword reaps the harvest of death; there is but one champion who can wear the papooshes of the elephant-slayer—it is Bobbachy Bahawder!"

"You speak truly, Puneeree Muckun, the Bahawder ruminates on the words of the unbeliever: he is an ostrich, and hatches the eggs of his thoughts."

"Bekhusm! on my nose be it! May the young birds, his actions, be strong and swift in flight."

"May they DIGEST IRON!" said Puneeree Muckun, who was evidently a wag in his way.

"O—ho!" thought I, as suddenly the light flashed upon me. "It was, then, the famous Bobbachy Bahawder whom I overcame just now! and he is the man destined to stand in my slippers, is he?" and I was at that very moment standing in his own! Such are the chances and changes that fall to the lot of the soldier!

I suppose everybody—everybody who has been in India, at least—has heard the name of Bobbachy Bahawder: it is derived from the two Hindustanee words—bobbachy, general; bahawder, artilleryman. He had entered into Holkar's service in the latter capacity, and had, by his merit and his undaunted bravery in action, attained the dignity of the peacock's feather, which is only granted to noblemen of the first class; he was married, moreover, to one of Holkar's innumerable daughters; a match which, according to the Chronique Scandaleuse, brought more of honour than of pleasure to the poor

Bobbachy. Gallant as he was in the field, it was said that in the harem he was the veriest craven alive, completely subjugated by his ugly and odious wife. In all matters of importance the late Bahawder had been consulted by his prince, who had, as it appears (knowing my character, and not caring to do anything rash in his attack upon so formidable an enemy), sent forward the unfortunate Pitan to reconnoitre the fort; he was to have done yet more, as I learned from the attendant Puneeree Muckun, who was, I soon found out, an old favourite with the Bobbachy—doubtless on account of his honesty and love of repartee.

"The Bahawder's lips are closed," said he, at last, trotting up to me; "has he not a word for old Puneeree Muckun?"

"Bismillah, mashallah, barikallah," said I; which means, "My good friend, what I have seen is not worth the trouble of relation, and fills my bosom with the darkest forebodings."

"You could not then see the Gujputi alone, and stab him with your dagger?"

[Here was a pretty conspiracy!] "No, I saw him, but not alone; his people were always with him."

"Hurrumzadeh! it is a pity; we waited but the sound of your jogree (whistle), and straightway would have galloped up and seized upon every man, woman, and child in the fort: however, there are but a dozen men in the garrison, and they have not provision for two days—they must yield; and then hurrah for the moon-faces! Mashallah! I am told the soldiers who first get in are to have their pick. How my old woman, Rotee Muckun, will be surprised when I bring home a couple of Feringhee wives,—ha! ha!"

"Fool!" said I, "be still!—twelve men in the garrison there are twelve hundred! Gahagan himself is as good as a thousand men; and as for food, I saw with my own eyes five hundred bullocks grazing in the courtyard as I entered." This WAS a bouncer, I confess; but my object was to deceive Puneeree Muckun, and give him as high a notion as possible of the capabilities of defence which the besieged had.

"Pooch, pooch," murmured the men; "it is a wonder of a fortress: we shall never be able to take it until our guns come up."

There was hope then! they had no battering-train. Ere this arrived I trusted that Lord Lake would hear of our plight, and march down to rescue us. Thus occupied in thought and conversation, we rode on until the advanced sentinel challenged us, when old Puneeree gave the word, and we passed on into the centre of Holkar's camp.

It was a strange—a stirring sight! The camp-fires were lighted; and round them—eating, reposing, talking, looking at the merry steps of the dancing-girls, or listening to the stories of some Dhol Baut (or Indian improvisatore)—were thousands of dusky soldiery. The camels and horses were picketed under the banyan- trees, on which the ripe mango fruit was growing, and offered them an excellent food. Towards the spot which the golden fish and royal purdahs, floating in the wind, designated as the tent of Holkar, led an immense avenue—of elephants! the finest street, indeed, I ever saw. Each of the monstrous animals had a castle on its back, armed with Mauritanian archers and the celebrated Persian matchlock-men: it was the feeding time of these royal brutes, and the grooms were observed bringing immense toffungs, or baskets, filled with pine-apples, plantains, bananas, Indian corn, and cocoa-nuts, which grow luxuriantly at all seasons of the year. We passed down this extraordinary avenue—no less than three hundred and eighty-eight tails did I count on each side—each tail appertaining to an elephant twenty-five feet high—each elephant having a two-storied castle on its back—each castle containing sleeping and eating rooms for the twelve men that formed its garrison, and were keeping watch on the roof—each roof bearing a flagstaff twenty feet long on its top, the crescent glittering with a thousand gems, and round it the imperial standard,—each standard of silk velvet and cloth-of-gold, bearing the well-known device of Holkar, argent an or gules, between a sinople of the first, a chevron truncated, wavy. I took nine of these myself in the course of a very short time after, and shall be happy, when I come to England, to show them to any gentleman who has a curiosity that way. Through this gorgeous scene our little cavalcade passed, and at last we arrived at the quarters occupied by Holkar.

That celebrated chieftain's tents and followers were gathered round one of the British bungalows which had escaped the flames, and which he occupied during the siege. When I entered the large room where he sat, I found him in the midst of a council of war; his chief generals and viziers seated round him, each smoking his hookah, as is the common way with these black fellows, before, at, and after breakfast, dinner, supper, and bedtime. There was such a cloud raised by their smoke you could hardly see a yard before you- -another piece of good-luck for me—as it diminished the chances of my detection. When, with the ordinary ceremonies, the kitmatgars and consomahs had explained to the prince that Bobbachy Bahawder, the right eye of the Sun of the Universe (as the ignorant heathens called me), had arrived from his mission, Holkar immediately summoned me to the maidaun, or elevated platform, on which he was seated in a luxurious easy-chair, and I, instantly taking off my slippers, falling on my knees, and beating my head against the ground ninety-nine times, proceeded, still on my knees, a hundred and twenty feet through the room, and then up the twenty steps which led to his maidaun—a silly, painful, and disgusting ceremony, which can only be considered as a relic of barbarian darkness, which tears the knees and shins to pieces, let alone the pantaloons. I recommend anybody who goes to India, with the prospect of entering the service of the native rajahs, to recollect my advice, and have them WELL WADDED.

Well, the right eye of the Sun of the Universe scrambled as well as he could up the steps of the maidaun (on which, in rows, smoking, as I have said, the musnuds or general officers were seated), and I arrived within speaking distance of Holkar, who instantly asked me the success of my mission. The impetuous old man thereon poured out a multitude of questions: "How many men are there in the fort?" said he; "how many women? Is it victualled? have they ammunition? Did you see Gahagan Sahib, the commander? did you kill him?"

All these questions Jeswunt Row Holkar puffed out with so many whiffs of tobacco.

Taking a chillum myself, and raising about me such a cloud that, upon my honour as a gentleman, no man at three yards' distance could perceive anything of me except the pillar of smoke in which I was encompassed, I told Holkar, in Oriental language of course, the best tale I could with regard to the fort.

"Sir," said I, "to answer your last question first—that dreadful Gujputi I have seen—and he is alive: he is eight feet, nearly, in height; he can eat a bullock daily (of which he has seven hundred at present in the compound, and swears that during the siege he will content himself with only three a week): he has lost, in battle, his left eye; and what is the consequence? O Ram Gunge" (O thou-with-the-eye-as-bright-as-morning and-with-beard-as-black-as- night), "Goliah Gujputi—NEVER SLEEPS!"

"Ah, you Ghorumsaug (you thief of the world)," said the Prince Vizier, Saadut Alee Beg Bimbukchee—"it's joking you are;"—and there was a universal buzz through the room at the announcement of this bouncer.

"By the hundred and eleven incarnations of Vishnu," said I, solemnly (an oath which no Indian was ever known to break), "I swear that so it is: so at least he told me, and I have good cause to know his power. Gujputi is an enchanter: he is leagued with devils; he is invulnerable. Look," said I, unsheathing my dagger— and every eye turned instantly towards me—"thrice did I stab him with this steel—in the back, once—twice right through the heart; but he only laughed me to scorn, and bade me tell Holkar that the steel was not yet forged which was to inflict an injury upon him."

I never saw a man in such a rage as Holkar was when I gave him this somewhat imprudent message.

"Ah, lily-livered rogue!" shouted he out to me, "milk-blooded unbeliever! pale-faced miscreant! lives he after insulting thy master in thy presence? In the name of the Prophet, I spit on thee, defy thee, abhor thee, degrade thee! Take that, thou liar of the universe! and that—and that—and that!"

Such are the frightful excesses of barbaric minds! every time this old man said, "Take that," he flung some article near him at the head of the undaunted Gahagan—his dagger, his sword, his carbine, his richly ornamented pistols, his turban covered with jewels, worth a hundred thousand crores of rupees— finally, his hookah, snake mouthpiece, silver-bell, chillum and all—which went hissing over my head, and flattening into a jelly the nose of the Grand Vizier.

"Yock muzzee! my nose is off," said the old man, mildly. "Will you have my life, O Holkar? it is thine likewise!" and no other word of complaint escaped his lips.

Of all these missiles, though a pistol and carbine had gone off as the ferocious Indian flung them at my head, and the naked scimitar, fiercely but unadroitly thrown, had lopped off the limbs of one or two of the musnuds as they sat trembling on their omrahs, yet, strange to say, not a single weapon had hurt me. When the hubbub ceased, and the unlucky wretches who had been the victims of this fit of rage had been removed, Holkar's good-humour somewhat returned, and he allowed me to continue my account of the fort; which I did, not taking the slightest notice of his burst of impatience: as indeed it would have been the height of impoliteness to have done, for such accidents happened many times in the day.

"It is well that the Bobbachy has returned," snuffled out the poor Grand Vizier, after I had explained to the Council the extraordinary means of defence possessed by the garrison.

"Your star is bright, O Bahawder! for this very night we had resolved upon an escalade of the fort, and we had sworn to put every one of the infidel garrison to the edge of the sword."

"But you have no battering train," said I.

"Bah! we have a couple of ninety-six pounders, quite sufficient to blow the gates open; and then, hey for a charge!" said Loll Mahommed, a general of cavalry, who was a rival of Bobbachy's, and contradicted, therefore, every word I said. "In the name of Juggernaut, why wait for the heavy artillery? Have we not swords? Have we not hearts? Mashallah! Let cravens stay with Bobbachy, all true men will follow Loll Mahommed! Allahhumdillah, Bismillah, Barikallah?" and drawing his scimitar, he waved it over his head, and shouted out his cry of battle. It was repeated by many of the other omrahs; the sound of their cheers was carried into the camp, and caught up by the men; the camels began to cry, the horses to prance and neigh, the eight hundred elephants set up a scream, the trumpeters and drummers clanged away at their instruments. I never heard such a din before or after. How I trembled for my little garrison when I heard the enthusiastic cries of this innumerable host!

There was but one way for it. "Sir," said I, addressing Holkar, "go out to-night, and you go to certain death. Loll Mahommed has not seen the fort as I have. Pass the gate if you please, and for what? to fall before the fire of a hundred pieces of artillery; to storm another gate, and then another, and then to be blown up, with Gahagan's garrison in the citadel. Who talks of courage? Were I not in your august presence, O star of the faithful, I would crop Loll Mahommed's nose from his face, and wear his ears as an ornament in my own pugree! Who is there here that knows not the difference between yonder yellow-skinned coward and Gahagan Khan Guj—I mean Bobbachy Bahawder? I am ready to fight one, two, three, or twenty of them, at broad-sword, small-sword, single- stick, with fists if you please. By the holy piper, fighting is like mate and dthrink to Ga—-to Bobbachy, I mane—whoop! come on, you divvle, and I'll bate the skin off your ugly bones."

This speech had very nearly proved fatal to me, for, when I am agitated, I involuntarily adopt some of the phraseology peculiar to my own country; which is so un-eastern, that, had there been any suspicion as to my real character, detection must indubitably have ensued. As it was, Holkar perceived nothing, but instantaneously stopped the dispute. Loll Mahommed, however, evidently suspected something; for, as Holkar, with a voice of thunder, shouted out; "Tomasha (silence)," Loll sprang forward and gasped out -

"My lord! my lord! this is not Bob—"

But he could say no more. "Gag the slave!" screamed out Holkar, stamping with fury; and a turban was instantly twisted round the poor devil's jaws. "Ho, furoshes! carry out Loll Mahommed Khan, give him a hundred dozen on the soles of his feet, set him upon a white donkey, and carry him round the camp, with an inscription before him: 'This is the way that Holkar rewards the talkative.'"

I breathed again; and ever as I heard each whack of the bamboo falling on Loll Mahommed's feet, I felt peace returning to my mind, and thanked my stars that I was delivered of this danger.

"Vizier," said Holkar, who enjoyed Loll's roars amazingly, "I owe you a reparation for your nose: kiss the hand of your prince, O Saadut Alee Beg Bimbukchee! be from this day forth Zoheir u Dowlut!"

The good old man's eyes filled with tears. "I can bear thy severity, O Prince," said he; "I cannot bear thy love. Was it not an honour that your Highness did me just now when you condescended to pass over the bridge of your slave's nose?"

The phrase was by all voices pronounced to be very poetical. The Vizier retired, crowned with his new honours, to bed. Holkar was in high good-humour.

"Bobbachy," said he, "thou, too, must pardon me. A propos, I have news for thee. Your wife, the incomparable Puttee Rooge" (white and red rose), "has arrived in camp."

"My WIFE, my lord!" said I, aghast.

"Our daughter, the light of thine eyes! Go, my son; I see thou art wild with joy. The Princess's tents are set up close by mine, and I know thou longest to join her."

My wife? Here was a complication truly!

CHAPTER V

THE ISSUE OF MY INTERVIEW WITH MY WIFE

I found Puneeree Muckun, with the rest of my attendants, waiting at the gate, and they immediately conducted me to my own tents in the neighbourhood. I have been in many dangerous predicaments before that time and since, but I don't care to deny that I felt in the present instance such a throbbing of the heart as I never have experienced when leading a forlorn hope, or marching up to a battery.

As soon as I entered the tents a host of menials sprang forward, some to ease me of my armour, some to offer me refreshments, some with hookahs, attar of roses (in great quart bottles), and the thousand delicacies of Eastern life. I motioned them away. "I will wear my armour," said I; "I shall go forth to-night. Carry my duty to the princess, and say I grieve that to-night I have not the time to see her. Spread me a couch here, and bring me supper here: a jar of Persian wine well cooled, a lamb stuffed with pistachio- nuts, a pillow of a couple of turkeys, a curried kid—anything. Begone! Give me a pipe; leave me alone, and tell me when the meal is ready."

I thought by these means to put off the fair Puttee Rooge, and hoped to be able to escape without subjecting myself to the examination of her curious eyes. After smoking for a while, an attendant came to tell me that my supper was prepared in the inner apartment of the tent (I suppose that the reader, if he be possessed of the commonest intelligence, knows that the tents of the Indian grandees are made of the finest Cashmere Shawls, and contain a dozen rooms at least, with carpets, chimneys, and sash-windows complete). I entered, I say, into an inner chamber, and there began with my fingers to devour my meal in the Oriental fashion, taking, every now and then, a pull from the wine-jar, which was cooling deliciously in another jar of snow.

I was just in the act of despatching the last morsel of a most savoury stewed lamb and rice, which had formed my meal, when I heard a scuffle of feet, a shrill clatter of female voices, and, the curtain being flung open, in marched a lady accompanied by twelve slaves, with moon faces and slim waists, lovely as the houris in Paradise.

The lady herself, to do her justice, was as great a contrast to her attendants as could possibly be: she was crooked, old, of the complexion of molasses, and rendered a thousand times more ugly by the tawdry dress and the blazing jewels with which she was covered. A line of yellow chalk drawn from her forehead to the tip of her nose (which was further ornamented by an immense glittering nose- ring), her eyelids painted bright red, and a large dab of the same colour on her chin, showed she was not of the Mussulman, but the Brahmin faith—and of a very high caste: you could see that by her eyes. My mind was instantaneously made up as to my line of action.

The male attendants had of course quitted the apartment, as they heard the well-known sound of her voice. It would have been death to them to have remained and looked in her face. The females ranged themselves round their mistress, as she squatted down opposite to me.

"And is this," said she, "a welcome, O Khan! after six months' absence, for the most unfortunate and loving wife in all the world? Is this lamb, O glutton! half so tender as thy spouse? Is this wine, O sot! half so sweet as her looks?"

I saw the storm was brewing—her slaves, to whom she turned, kept up a kind of chorus:-

"Oh, the faithless one!" cried they. "Oh, the rascal, the false one, who has no eye for beauty, and no heart for love, like the Khanum's!"

"A lamb is not so sweet as love," said I gravely; "but a lamb has a good temper: a wine-cup is not so intoxicating as a woman—but a wine-cup has NO TONGUE, O Khanum Gee!" and again I dipped my nose in the soul-refreshing jar.

The sweet Puttee Rooge was not, however, to be put off by my repartees; she and her maidens recommenced their chorus, and chattered and stormed until I lost all patience.

"Retire, friends," said I, "and leave me in peace."

"Stir, on your peril!" cried the Khanum.

So, seeing there was no help for it but violence, I drew out my pistols, cocked them, and said, "O houris! these pistols contain each two balls: the daughter of Holkar bears a sacred life for me- -but for you!—by all the saints of Hindustan, four of ye shall die if ye stay a moment longer in my presence!" This was enough; the ladies gave a shriek, and skurried out of the apartment like a covey of partridges on the wing.

Now, then, was the time for action. My wife, or rather Bobbachy's wife, sat still, a little flurried by the unusual ferocity which her lord had displayed in her presence. I seized her hand and, gripping it close, whispered in her ear, to which I put the other pistol:- "O Khanum, listen and scream not; the moment you scream, you die!" She was completely beaten: she turned as pale as a woman could in her situation, and said, "Speak, Bobbachy Bahawder, I am dumb."

"Woman," said I, taking off my helmet, and removing the chain cape which had covered almost the whole of my face—"I AM NOT THY HUSBAND—I am the slayer of elephants, the world-renowned GAHAGAN!"

As I said this, and as the long ringlets of red hair fell over my shoulders (contrasting strangely with my dyed face and beard), I formed one of the finest pictures that can possibly be conceived, and I recommend it as a subject to Mr. Heath, for the next "Book of Beauty."

"Wretch!" said she, "what wouldst thou?"

"You black-faced fiend," said I, "raise but your voice, and you are dead!"

"And afterwards," said she, "do you suppose that YOU can escape? The torments of hell are not so terrible as the tortures that Holkar will invent for thee."

"Tortures, madam?" answered I, coolly. "Fiddlesticks! You will neither betray me, nor will I be put to the torture: on the contrary, you will give me your best jewels and facilitate my escape to the fort. Don't grind your teeth and swear at me. Listen, madam: you know this dress and these arms;—they are the arms of your husband, Bobbachy Bahawder—MY PRISONER. He now lies in yonder fort, and if I do not return before daylight, at sunrise he dies: and then, when they send his corpse back to Holkar, what will you, his WIDOW, do?

"Oh!" said she, shuddering, "spare me, spare me!"

"I'll tell you what you will do. You will have the pleasure of dying along with him—of BEING ROASTED, madam: an agonising death, from which your father cannot save you, to which he will be the first man to condemn and conduct you. Ha! I see we understand each other, and you will give me over the cash-box and jewels." And so saying I threw myself back with the calmest air imaginable, flinging the pistols over to her. "Light me a pipe, my love," said I, "and then go and hand me over the dollars: do you hear?" You see I had her in my power—up a tree, as the Americans say, and she very humbly lighted my pipe for me, and then departed for the goods I spoke about.

What a thing is luck! If Loll Mahommed had not been made to take that ride round the camp, I should infallibly have been lost.

My supper, my quarrel with the princess, and my pipe afterwards, had occupied a couple of hours of my time. The princess returned from her quest, and brought with her the box, containing valuables to the amount of about three millions sterling. (I was cheated of them afterwards, but have the box still, a plain deal one.) I was just about to take my departure, when a tremendous knocking, shouting, and screaming was heard at the entrance of the tent. It was Holkar himself, accompanied by that cursed Loll Mahommed, who, after his punishment, found his master restored to good-humour, and had communicated to him his firm conviction that I was an impostor.

"Ho, Begum!" shouted he, in the ante-room (for he and his people could not enter the women's apartments), "speak, O my daughter! is your husband returned?"

"Speak, madam," said I, "or REMEMBER THE ROASTING."

"He is, Papa," said the Begum.

"Are you sure? Ho! ho! ho!" (the old ruffian was laughing outside)—"are you sure it is?—Ha! aha!—he-e-e!"

"Indeed it is he, and no other. I pray you, father, to go, and to pass no more such shameless jests on your daughter. Have I ever seen the face of any other man?" And hereat she began to weep as if her heart would break—the deceitful minx!

Holkar's laugh was instantly turned to fury. "Oh, you liar and eternal thief!" said he, turning round (as I presume, for I could only hear) to Loll Mahommed, "to make your prince eat such monstrous dirt as this! Furoshes, seize this man. I dismiss him from my service, I degrade him from his rank, I appropriate to myself all his property: and hark ye, furoshes, GIVE HIM A HUNDRED DOZEN MORE!"

Again I heard the whacks of the bamboos, and peace flowed into my soul.

Just as morn began to break, two figures were seen to approach the little fortress of Futtyghur: one was a woman wrapped closely in a veil; the other a warrior, remarkable for the size and manly beauty of his form, who carried in his hand a deal box of considerable size. The warrior at the gate gave the word and was admitted; the woman returned slowly to the Indian camp. Her name was Puttee Rooge; his was -

G. O'G. G., M.H.E.I.C.S.. C.I.H.A.

CHAPTER VI

FAMINE IN THE GARRISON

Thus my dangers for the night being overcome, I hastened with my precious box into my own apartment, which communicated with another, where I had left my prisoner, with a guard to report if he should recover, and to prevent his escape. My servant, Ghorumsaug, was one of the guard. I called him, and the fellow came, looking very much confused and frightened, as it seemed, at my appearance.

"Why, Ghorumsaug," said I, "what makes thee look so pale, fellow?" (He was as white as a sheet.) "It is thy master, dost thou not remember him?" The man had seen me dress myself in the Pitan's clothes, but was not present when I had blacked my face and beard in the manner I have described.

"O Bramah, Vishnu, and Mahomet!" cried the faithful fellow, "and do I see my dear master disguised in this way? For Heaven's sake let me rid you of this odious black paint; for what will the ladies say in the ballroom, if the beautiful Feringhee should appear amongst them with his roses turned into coal?"

I am still one of the finest men in Europe, and at the time of which I write, when only two-and-twenty, I confess I was a little vain of my personal appearance, and not very willing to appear before my dear Belinda disguised like a blackamoor. I allowed Ghorumsaug to divest me of the heathenish armour and habiliments which I wore; and having, with a world of scrubbing and trouble, divested my face and beard of their black tinge, I put on my own becoming uniform, and hastened to wait on the ladies; hastened, I say,—although delayed would have been the better word, for the operation of bleaching lasted at least two hours.

"How is the prisoner, Ghorumsaug?" said I, before leaving my apartment.

"He has recovered from the blow which the Lion dealt him; two men and myself watch over him; and Macgillicuddy Sahib (the second in command) has just been the rounds, and has seen that all was secure."

I bade Ghorumsaug help me to put away my chest of treasure (my exultation in taking it was so great that I could not help informing him of its contents); and this done, I despatched him to his post near the prisoner, while I prepared to sally forth and pay my respects to the fair creatures under my protection. "What good after all have I done," thought I to myself, "in this expedition which I had so rashly undertaken?" I had seen the renowned Holkar; I had been in the heart of his camp; I knew the disposition of his troops, that there were eleven thousand of them, and that he only waited for his guns to make a regular attack on the fort. I had seen Puttee Rooge; I had robbed her (I say ROBBED her, and I don't care what the reader or any other man may think of the act) of a deal box, containing jewels to the amount of three millions sterling, the property of herself and husband.

Three millions in money and jewels! And what the deuce were money and jewels to me or to my poor garrison? Could my adorable Miss Bulcher eat a fricassee of diamonds, or, Cleopatra-like, melt down pearls to her tea? Could I, careless as I am about food, with a stomach that would digest anything— (once, in Spain, I ate the leg of a horse during a famine, and was so eager to swallow this morsel that I bolted the shoe, as well as the hoof, and never felt the slightest inconvenience from either)—could I, I say, expect to live long and well upon a ragout of rupees, or a dish of stewed emeralds and rubies? With all the wealth of Croesus before me I felt melancholy; and would have paid cheerfully its weight in carats for a good honest round of boiled beef. Wealth, wealth, what art thou? What is gold?—Soft metal. What are diamonds?— Shining tinsel. The great wealth-winners, the only fame-achievers, the sole objects worthy of a soldier's consideration, are beefsteaks, gunpowder, and cold iron.

The two latter means of competency we possessed; I had in my own apartments a small store of gunpowder (keeping it under my own bed, with a candle burning for fear of accidents); I had 14 pieces of artillery (4 long 48's and 4 carronades, 5 howitzers, and a long brass mortar, for grape, which I had taken myself at the battle of Assaye), and muskets for ten times my force. My garrison, as I have told the reader in a previous number, consisted of 40 men, two chaplains, and a surgeon; add to these my guests, 83 in number, of whom nine only were gentlemen (in tights, powder, pigtails, and silk stockings, who had come out merely for a dance, and found themselves in for a siege). Such were our numbers:-

Troops and artillerymen	40
Ladies	74
Other non-combatants	11
MAJOR-GENERAL O'G.GAHAGAN	1,000
	1,125

I count myself good for a thousand, for so I was regularly rated in the army: with this great benefit to it, that I only consumed as much as an ordinary mortal. We were then, as far as the victuals went, 126 mouths; as combatants we numbered 1,040 gallant men, with 12 guns and a fort, against Holkar and his 12,000. No such alarming odds, if -

IF!—ay, there was the rub—IF we had SHOT, as well as powder for our guns; IF we had not only MEN but MEAT. Of the former commodity we had only three rounds for each piece. Of the latter, upon my sacred honour, to feed 126 souls, we had but

Two drumsticks of fowls, and a bone of ham. Fourteen bottles of ginger-beer. Of soda-water, four ditto. Two bottles of fine Spanish olives. Raspberry cream—the remainder of two dishes. Seven macaroons, lying in the puddle of a demolished trifle. Half a drum of best Turkey figs. Some bits of broken bread; two Dutch cheeses (whole); the crust of an old Stilton; and about an ounce of almonds and raisins. Three ham-sandwiches, and a pot of currant-jelly, and 197 bottles of brandy, rum, madeira, pale ale (my private stock); a couple of hard eggs for a salad, and a flask of Florence oil.

This was the provision for the whole garrison! The men after supper had seized upon the relics of the repast, as they were carried off from the table; and these were the miserable remnants I found and counted on my return; taking good care to lock the door of the supper-room, and treasure what little sustenance still remained in it.

When I appeared in the saloon, now lighted up by the morning sun, I not only caused a sensation myself, but felt one in my own bosom which was of the most painful description. Oh, my reader! may you never behold such a sight as that which presented itself: eighty- three men and women in ball-dresses; the former with their lank powdered locks streaming over their faces; the latter with faded flowers, uncurled wigs, smudged rouge, blear eyes, draggling feathers, rumpled satins—each more desperately melancholy and hideous than the other—each, except my beloved Belinda Bulcher, whose raven ringlets never having been in curl could of course never go out of curl; whose cheek, pale as the lily, could, as it may naturally be supposed, grow no paler; whose neck and beauteous arms, dazzling as alabaster, needed no pearl-powder, and therefore, as I need not state, did not suffer because the pearl-powder had come off. Joy (deft link-boy!) lit his lamps in each of her eyes as I entered. As if I had been her sun, her spring, lo! blushing roses mantled in her cheek! Seventy-three ladies, as I entered, opened their fire upon me, and stunned me with cross-questions, regarding my adventures in the camp—SHE, as she saw me, gave a faint scream (the sweetest, sure, that ever gurgled through the throat of a woman!) then started up—then made as if she would sit down—then moved backwards—then tottered forwards—then tumbled into my—Psha! why recall, why attempt to describe that delicious— that passionate greeting of two young hearts? What was the surrounding crowd to us? What cared we for the sneers of the men, the titters of the jealous women, the shrill "Upon my word!" of the elder Miss Bulcher, and the loud expostulations of Belinda's mamma? The brave girl loved me, and wept in my arms. "Goliah! my Goliah!" said she, "my brave, my beautiful, THOU art returned, and hope comes back with thee. Oh! who can tell the anguish of my soul, during this dreadful dreadful night!" Other similar ejaculations of love and joy she uttered; and if I HAD perilled life in her service, if I DID believe that hope of escape there was none, so exquisite was the moment of our meeting, that I forgot all else in this overwhelming joy!

[The Major's description of this meeting, which lasted at the very most not ten seconds, occupies thirteen pages of writing. We have been compelled to dock off twelve-and-a-half; for the whole passage, though highly creditable to his feelings, might possibly be tedious to the reader.]

As I said, the ladies and gentlemen were inclined to sneer, and were giggling audibly. I led the dear girl to a chair, and, scowling round with a tremendous fierceness, which those who know me know I can sometimes put on, I shouted out, "Hark ye! men and women—I am this lady's truest knight—her husband I hope one day to be. I am commander, too, in this fort—the enemy is without it; another word of mockery—another glance of scorn—and, by Heaven, I will hurl every man and woman from the battlements, a prey to the ruffianly Holkar!" This quieted them. I am a man of my word, and none of them stirred or looked disrespectfully from that moment.

It was now my turn to make them look foolish. Mrs. Vandegobbleschroy (whose unfailing appetite is pretty well known to every person who has been in India) cried, "Well, Captain Gahagan, your ball has been so pleasant, and the supper was despatched so long ago, that myself and the ladies would be very glad of a little breakfast." And Mrs. Van giggled as if she had made a very witty and reasonable speech. "Oh! breakfast, breakfast, by all means," said the rest; "we really are dying for a warm cup of tea."

"Is it bohay tay or souchong tay that you'd like, ladies?" says I.

"Nonsense, you silly man; any tea you like," said fat Mrs. Van.

"What do you say, then, to some prime GUNPOWDER?" Of course they said it was the very thing.

"And do you like hot rowls or cowld—muffins or crumpets—fresh butter or salt? And you, gentlemen, what do you say to some ilegant divvled-kidneys for yourselves, and just a trifle of grilled turkeys, and a couple of hundthred new-laid eggs for the ladies?"

"Pooh, pooh! be it as you will, my dear fellow," answered they all.

"But stop," says I. "O ladies, O ladies! O gentlemen, gentlemen! that you should ever have come to the quarters of Goliah Gahagan, and he been without—"

"What?" said they, in a breath.

"Alas! alas! I have not got a single stick of chocolate in the whole house."

"Well, well, we can do without it."

"Or a single pound of coffee."

"Never mind; let that pass too." (Mrs. Van and the rest were beginning to look alarmed.)

"And about the kidneys—now I remember, the black divvles outside the fort have seized upon all the sheep; and how are we to have kidneys without them?" (Here there was a slight o-o-o!)

"And with regard to the milk and crame, it may be remarked that the cows are likewise in pawn, and not a single drop can be had for money or love: but we can beat up eggs, you know, in the tay, which will be just as good."

"Oh! just as good."

"Only the divvle's in the luck, there's not a fresh egg to be had— no, nor a fresh chicken," continued I, "nor a stale one either; not a tayspoonful of souchong, nor a thimbleful of bohay; nor the laste taste in life of butther, salt or fresh; nor hot rowls or cowld!"

"In the name of Heaven!" said Mrs. Van, growing very pale, "what is there, then?"

"Ladies and gentlemen, I'll tell you what there is now," shouted I. "There's

"Two drumsticks of fowls, and a bone of ham. Fourteen bottles of ginger-beer," &c. &c. &c.

And I went through the whole list of eatables as before, ending with the ham-sandwiches and the pot of jelly.

"Law! Mr. Gahagan," said Mrs. Colonel Vandegobbleschroy, "give me the ham-sandwiches—I must manage to breakfast off them."

And you should have heard the pretty to-do there was at this modest proposition! Of course I did not accede to it—why should I? I was the commander of the fort, and intended to keep these three very sandwiches for the use of myself and my dear Belinda. "Ladies," said I, "there are in this fort one hundred and twenty- six souls, and this is all the food which is to last us during the siege. Meat there is none—of drink there is a tolerable quantity; and at one o'clock punctually, a glass of wine and one olive shall be served out to each woman: the men will receive two glasses, and an olive and a fig—and this must be your food during the siege. Lord Lake cannot be absent more than three days; and if he be— why, still there is a chance—why do I say a chance?—a CERTAINTY of escaping from the hands of these ruffians."

"Oh, name it, name it, dear Captain Gahagan!" screeched the whole covey at a breath.

"It lies," answered I, "in the powder magazine. I will blow this fort, and all it contains, to atoms, ere it becomes the prey of Holkar."

The women, at this, raised a squeal that might have been heard in Holkar's camp, and fainted in different directions; but my dear Belinda whispered in my ear, "Well done, thou noble knight! bravely said, my heart's Goliah!" I felt I was right: I could have blown her up twenty times for the luxury of that single moment! "And now, ladies," said I, "I must leave you. The two chaplains will remain with you to administer professional consolation—the other gentlemen will follow me upstairs to the ramparts, where I shall find plenty of work for them."

CHAPTER VII

THE ESCAPE

Loth as they were, these gentlemen had nothing for it but to obey, and they accordingly followed me to the ramparts, where I proceeded to review my men. The fort, in my absence, had been left in command of Lieutenant Macgillicuddy, a countryman of my own (with whom, as may be seen in an early chapter of my memoirs, I had an affair of honour); and the prisoner Bobbachy Bahawder, whom I had only stunned, never wishing to kill him, had been left in charge of that officer. Three of the garrison (one of them a man of the Ahmednuggar Irregulars, my own body-servant, Ghorumsaug above named) were appointed to watch the captive by turns, and never leave him out of their sight. The lieutenant was instructed to look to them and to their prisoner; and as Bobbachy was severely injured by the blow which I had given him, and was, moreover, bound hand and foot, and gagged smartly with cords, I considered myself sure of his person.

Macgillicuddy did not make his appearance when I reviewed my little force, and the three havildars were likewise absent: this did not surprise me, as I had told them not to leave their prisoner; but desirous to speak with the lieutenant, I despatched a messenger to him, and ordered him to appear immediately.

The messenger came back; he was looking ghastly pale: he whispered some information into my ear, which instantly caused me to hasten to the apartments where I had caused Bobbachy Bahawder to be confined.

The men had fled;—Bobbachy had fled; and in his place, fancy my astonishment when I found—with a rope cutting his naturally wide mouth almost into his ears—with a dreadful sabre-cut across his forehead—with his legs tied over his head, and his arms tied between his legs—my unhappy, my attached friend—Mortimer Macgillicuddy!

He had been in this position for about three hours—it was the very position in which I had caused Bobbachy Bahawder to be placed—an attitude uncomfortable, it is true, but one which renders escape impossible, unless treason aid the prisoner.

I restored the lieutenant to his natural erect position; I poured half-a-bottle of whisky down the immensely enlarged orifice of his mouth; and when he had been released, he informed me of the circumstances that had taken place.

Fool that I was! idiot!—upon my return to the fort, to have been anxious about my personal appearance, and to have spent a couple of hours in removing the artificial blackening from my beard and complexion, instead of going to examine my prisoner—when his escape would have been prevented. O foppery, foppery!—it was that cursed love of personal appearance which had led me to forget my duty to my general, my country, my monarch, and my own honour!

Thus it was that the escape took place:- My own fellow of the Irregulars, whom I had summoned to dress me, performed the operation to my satisfaction, invested me with the elegant uniform of my corps, and removed the Pitan's disguise, which I had taken from the back of the prostrate Bobbachy Bahawder. What did the rogue do next?—Why, he carried back the dress to the Bobbachy—he put it, once more, on its right owner; he and his infernal black companions (who had been won over by the Bobbachy with promises of enormous reward) gagged Macgillicuddy, who was going the rounds, and then marched with the Indian coolly up to the outer gate, and gave the word. The sentinel, thinking it was myself, who had first come in, and was as likely to go out again—(indeed my rascally valet said that Gahagan Sahib was about to go out with him and his two companions to reconnoitre)—opened the gates, and off they went!

This accounted for the confusion of my valet when I entered!—and for the scoundrel's speech, that the lieutenant had JUST BEEN THE ROUNDS;—he HAD, poor fellow, and had been seized and bound in this cruel way. The three men, with their liberated prisoner, had just been on the point of escape, when my arrival disconcerted them: I had changed the guard at the gate (whom they had won over likewise); and yet, although they had overcome poor Mac, and although they were ready for the start, they had positively no means for effecting their escape, until I was ass enough to put means in their way. Fool! fool! thrice besotted fool that I was, to think of my own silly person when I should have been occupied solely with my public duty.

From Macgillicuddy's incoherent accounts, as he was gasping from the effects of the gag and the whisky he had taken to revive him, and from my own subsequent observations, I learned this sad story. A sudden and painful thought struck me—my precious box!—I rushed back, I found that box—I have it still. Opening it, there, where I had left ingots, sacks of bright tomauns, kopeks and rupees, strings of diamonds as big as ducks' eggs, rubies as red as the lips of my Belinda, countless strings of pearls, amethysts, emeralds, piles upon piles of bank-notes—I found—a piece of paper! with a few lines in the Sanscrit language, which are thus, word for word, translated:-

"EPIGRAM. (On disappointing a certain Major.)

"The conquering lion return'd with his prey, And safe in his cavern he set it; The sly little fox stole the booty away, And, as he escaped, to the lion did say, 'AHA! don't you wish you may get it?'"

Confusion! Oh, how my blood boiled as I read these cutting lines. I stamped,—I swore,—I don't know to what insane lengths my rage might have carried me, had not at this moment a soldier rushed in, screaming, "The enemy, the enemy!"

CHAPTER VIII

THE CAPTIVE

It was high time, indeed, that I should make my appearance. Waving my sword with one hand and seizing my telescope with the other, I at once frightened and examined the enemy. Well they knew when they saw that flamingo-plume floating in the breeze—that awful figure standing in the breach—that waving war-sword sparkling in the sky—well, I say, they knew the name of the humble individual who owned the sword, the plume, and the figure. The ruffians were mustered in front, the cavalry behind. The flags were flying, the drums, gongs, tambourines, violoncellos, and other instruments of Eastern music, raised in the air a strange barbaric melody; the officers (yatabals), mounted on white dromedaries, were seen galloping to and fro, carrying to the advancing hosts the orders of Holkar.

You see that two sides of the fort of Futtyghur (rising as it does on a rock that is almost perpendicular) are defended by the Burrumpooter river, two hundred feet deep at this point, and a thousand yards wide, so that I had no fear about them attacking me in that quarter. My guns, therefore (with their six-and-thirty miserable charges of shot), were dragged round to the point at which I conceived Holkar would be most likely to attack me. I was in a situation that I did not dare to fire, except at such times as I could kill a hundred men by a single discharge of a cannon; so the attacking party marched and marched, very strongly, about a mile and a half off, the elephants marching without receiving the slightest damage from us, until they had come to within four hundred yards of our walls (the rogues knew all the secrets of our weakness, through the betrayal of the dastardly Ghorumsaug, or they never would have ventured so near). At that distance—it was about the spot where the Futtyghur hill began gradually to rise—the invading force stopped; the elephants drew up in a line, at right angles with our wall (the fools! they thought they should expose themselves too much by taking a position parallel to it); the cavalry halted too, and—after the deuce's own flourish of trumpets and banging of gongs, to be sure,—somebody, in a flame-coloured satin dress, with an immense jewel blazing in his pugree (that looked through my telescope like a small but very bright planet), got up from the back of one of the very biggest elephants, and began a speech.

The elephants were, as I said, in a line formed with admirable precision, about three hundred of them. The following little diagram will explain matters:-

.... G | E | | F

E is the line of elephants. F is the wall of the fort. G a gun in the fort. Now the reader will see what I did.

The elephants were standing, their trunks waggling to and fro gracefully before them; and I, with superhuman skill and activity, brought the gun G (a devilish long brass gun) to bear upon them. I pointed it myself; bang! it went, and what was the consequence? Why, this:-

x .... G | E | | F

F is the fort, as before. G is the gun, as before. E, the elephants, as we have previously seen them. What then is x? x is the line taken by the ball fired from G, which took off ONE HUNDRED AND THIRTY-FOUR ELEPHANTS' TRUNKS, and only spent itself in the tusk of a very old animal, that stood the hundred and thirty-fifth!

I say that such a shot was never fired before or since; that a gun was never pointed in such a way. Suppose I had been a common man, and contented myself with firing bang at the head of the first animal? An ass would have done it, prided himself had he hit his mark, and what would have been the consequence? Why, that the ball might have killed two elephants and wounded a third; but here, probably, it would have stopped, and done no further mischief. The trunk was the place at which to aim; there are no bones there; and away, consequently, went the bullet, shearing, as I have said, through one hundred and thirty-five probosces. Heavens! what a howl there was when the shot took effect! What a sudden stoppage of Holkar's speech! What a hideous snorting of elephants! What a rush backwards was made by the whole army, as if some demon was pursuing them!

Away they went. No sooner did I see them in full retreat, than, rushing forward myself, I shouted to my men, "My friends, yonder lies your dinner!" We flung open the gates—we tore down to the spot where the elephants had fallen: seven of them were killed; and of those that escaped to die of their hideous wounds elsewhere, most had left their trunks behind them. A great quantity of them we seized; and I myself, cutting up with my scimitar a couple of the fallen animals, as a butcher would a calf, motioned to the men to take the pieces back to the fort, where barbecued elephant was served round for dinner, instead of the miserable allowance of an olive and a glass of wine, which I had promised to my female friends, in my speech to them. The animal reserved for the ladies was a young white one—the fattest and tenderest I ever ate in my life: they are very fair eating, but the flesh has an India-rubber flavour, which, until one is accustomed to it, is unpalatable.

It was well that I had obtained this supply, for, during my absence on the works, Mrs. Vandegobbleschroy and one or two others had forced their way into the supper-room, and devoured every morsel of the garrison larder, with the exception of the cheeses, the olives, and the wine, which were locked up in my own apartment, before which stood a sentinel. Disgusting Mrs. Van! When I heard of her gluttony, I had almost a mind to eat HER. However, we made a very comfortable dinner off the barbecued steaks, and when everybody had done, had the comfort of knowing that there was enough for one meal more.

The next day, as I expected, the enemy attacked us in great force, attempting to escalade the fort; but by the help of my guns, and my good sword, by the distinguished bravery of Lieutenant Macgillicuddy and the rest of the garrison, we beat this attack off completely, the enemy sustaining a loss of seven hundred men. We were victorious; but when another attack was made, what were we to do? We had still a little powder left, but had fired off all the shot, stones, iron-bars, &c. in the garrison! On this day, too, we devoured the last morsel of our food: I shall never forget Mrs. Vandegobbleschroy's despairing look, as I saw her sitting alone, attempting to make some impression on the little white elephant's roasted tail.

The third day the attack was repeated. The resources of genius are never at an end. Yesterday I had no ammunition; to-day, I discovered charges sufficient for two guns, and two swivels, which were much longer, but had bores of about blunderbuss size.

This time my friend Loll Mahommed, who had received, as the reader may remember, such a bastinadoing for my sake, headed the attack. The poor wretch could not walk, but he was carried in an open palanquin, and came on waving his sword, and cursing horribly in his Hindustan jargon. Behind him came troops of matchlock-men, who picked off every one of our men who showed their noses above the ramparts; and a great host of blackamoors with scaling-ladders, bundles to fill the ditch, fascines, gabions, culverins, demilunes, counterscarps, and all the other appurtenances of offensive war.

On they came; my guns and men were ready for them. You will ask how my pieces were loaded? I answer, that though my garrison were without food, I knew my duty as an officer, and HAD PUT THE TWO DUTCH CHEESES INTO THE TWO GUNS, AND HAD CRAMMED THE CONTENTS OF A BOTTLE OF OLIVES INTO EACH SWIVEL.

They advanced,—whish! went one of the Dutch cheeses,—bang! went the other. Alas! they did little execution. In their first contact with an opposing body, they certainly floored it; but they became at once like so much Welsh-rabbit, and did no execution beyond the man whom they struck down.

"Hogree, pogree, wongree-fum (praise to Allah and the forty-nine Imaums!)" shouted out the ferocious Loll Mahommed when he saw the failure of my shot. "Onward, sons of the Prophet! the infidel has no more ammunition. A hundred thousand lakhs of rupees to the man who brings me Gahagan's head!"

His men set up a shout, and rushed forward—he, to do him justice, was at the very head, urging on his own palanquin-bearers, and poking them with the tip of his scimitar. They came panting up the hill: I was black with rage, but it was the cold concentrated rage of despair. "Macgillicuddy," said I, calling that faithful officer, "you know where the barrels of powder are?" He did. "You know the use to make of them?" He did. He grasped my hand. "Goliah," said he, "farewell! I swear that the fort shall be in atoms, as soon as yonder unbelievers have carried it. Oh, my poor mother!" added the gallant youth, as sighing, yet fearless, he retired to his post.

I gave one thought to my blessed, my beautiful Belinda, and then, stepping into the front, took down one of the swivels;—a shower of matchlock balls came whizzing round my head. I did not heed them.

I took the swivel, and aimed coolly. Loll Mahommed, his palanquin, and his men, were now not above two hundred yards from the fort. Loll was straight before me, gesticulating and shouting to his men. I fired—bang!!!

I aimed so true, that ONE HUNDRED AND SEVENTEEN BEST SPANISH OLIVES WERE LODGED IN A LUMP IN THE FACE OF THE UNHAPPY LOLL MAHOMMED. The wretch, uttering a yell the most hideous and unearthly I ever heard, fell back dead; the frightened bearers flung down the palanquin and ran—the whole host ran as one man: their screams might be heard for leagues. "Tomasha, tomasha," they cried, "it is enchantment!" Away they fled, and the victory a third time was ours. Soon as the fight was done, I flew back to my Belinda. We had eaten nothing for twenty-four hours, but I forgot hunger in the thought of once more beholding her!

The sweet soul turned towards me with a sickly smile as I entered, and almost fainted in my arms; but alas! it was not love which caused in her bosom an emotion so strong—it was hunger! "Oh! my Goliah," whispered she, "for three days I have not tasted food—I could not eat that horrid elephant yesterday; but now—oh! Heaven!—" She could say no more, but sank almost lifeless on my shoulder. I administered to her a trifling dram of rum, which revived her for a moment, and then rushed downstairs, determined that if it were a piece of my own leg, she should still have something to satisfy her hunger. Luckily I remembered that three or four elephants were still lying in the field, having been killed by us in the first action, two days before. Necessity, thought I, has no law; my adorable girl must eat elephant, until she can get something better.

I rushed into the court where the men were, for the most part, assembled. "Men," said I, "our larder is empty; we must fill it as we did the day before yesterday. Who will follow Gahagan on a foraging party?" I expected that, as on former occasions, every man would offer to accompany me.

To my astonishment, not a soul moved—a murmur arose among the troops; and at last one of the oldest and bravest came forward.

"Captain," he said, "it is of no use; we cannot feed upon elephants for ever; we have not a grain of powder left, and must give up the fort when the attack is made to-morrow. We may as well be prisoners now as then, and we won't go elephant-hunting any more."

"Ruffian!" I said, "he who first talks of surrender, dies!" and I cut him down. "Is there anyone else who wishes to speak?"

No one stirred.

"Cowards! miserable cowards!" shouted I; "what, you dare not move for fear of death at the hands of those wretches who even now fled before your arms—what, do I say your arms?—before MINE!—alone I did it; and as alone I routed the foe, alone I will victual the fortress! Ho! open the gate!"

I rushed out; not a single man would follow. The bodies of the elephants that we had killed still lay on the ground where they had fallen, about four hundred yards from the fort. I descended calmly the hill, a very steep one, and coming to the spot, took my pick of the animals, choosing a tolerably small and plump one, of about thirteen feet high, which the vultures had respected. I threw this animal over my shoulders, and made for the fort.

As I marched up the acclivity, whizz—piff—whirr! came the balls over my head; and pitter-patter, pitter-patter! they fell on the body of the elephant like drops of rain. The enemy were behind me; I knew it, and quickened my pace. I heard the gallop of their horse: they came nearer, nearer; I was within a hundred yards of the fort—seventy—fifty! I strained every nerve; I panted with the superhuman exertion—I ran—could a man run very fast with such a tremendous weight on his shoulders?

Up came the enemy; fifty horsemen were shouting and screaming at my tail. O Heaven! five yards more—one moment—and I am saved. It is done—I strain the last strain—I make the last step—I fling forward my precious burden into the gate opened wide to receive me and it, and—I fall! The gate thunders to, and I am left on the outside! Fifty knives are gleaming before my bloodshot eyes—fifty black hands are at my throat, when a voice exclaims, "Stop!—kill him not, it is Gujputi!" A film came over my eyes—exhausted nature would bear no more.

CHAPTER IX

SURPRISE OF FUTTYGHUR

When I awoke from the trance into which I had fallen, I found myself in a bath, surrounded by innumerable black faces; and a Hindoo pothukoor (whence our word apothecary) feeling my pulse and looking at me with an air of sagacity.

"Where am I?" I exclaimed, looking round and examining the strange faces, and the strange apartment which met my view. "Bekhusm!" said the apothecary. "Silence! Gahagan Sahib is in the hands of those who know his valour, and will save his life."

"Know my valour, slave? Of course you do," said I; "but the fort— the garrison—the elephant—Belinda, my love—my darling— Macgillicuddy—the scoundrelly mutineers—the deal bo- "

I could say no more; the painful recollections pressed so heavily upon my poor shattered mind and frame, that both failed once more. I fainted again, and I know not how long I lay insensible.

Again, however, I came to my senses: the pothukoor applied restoratives, and after a slumber of some hours I awoke, much refreshed. I had no wound; my repeated swoons had been brought on (as indeed well they might) by my gigantic efforts in carrying the elephant up a steep hill a quarter of a mile in length. Walking, the task is bad enough: but running, it is the deuce; and I would recommend any of my readers who may be disposed to try and carry a dead elephant, never, on any account, to go a pace of more than five miles an hour.

Scarcely was I awake, when I heard the clash of arms at my door (plainly indicating that sentinels were posted there), and a single old gentleman, richly habited, entered the room. Did my eyes deceive me? I had surely seen him before. No—yes—no—yes—it was he: the snowy white beard, the mild eyes, the nose flattened to a jelly, and level with the rest of the venerable face, proclaimed him at once to be— Saadut Alee Beg Bimbukchee, Holkar's Prime Vizier; whose nose, as the reader may recollect, his Highness had flattened with his kaleawn during my interview with him in the Pitan's disguise. I now knew my fate but too well—I was in the hands of Holkar.

Saadut Alee Beg Bimbukchee slowly advanced towards me, and with a mild air of benevolence which distinguished that excellent man (he was torn to pieces by wild horses the year after, on account of a difference with Holkar), he came to my bedside and, taking gently my hand, said, "Life and death, my son, are not ours. Strength is deceitful, valour is unavailing, fame is only wind—the nightingale sings of the rose all night—where is the rose in the morning? Booch, booch! it is withered by a frost. The rose makes remarks regarding the nightingale, and where is that delightful song-bird? Pena-bekhoda, he is netted, plucked, spitted, and roasted! Who knows how misfortune comes? It has come to Gahagan Gujputi!"

"It is well," said I, stoutly, and in the Malay language. "Gahagan Gujputi will bear it like a man."

"No doubt—like a wise man and a brave one; but there is no lane so long to which there is not a turning, no night so black to which there comes not a morning. Icy winter is followed by merry springtime—grief is often succeeded by joy."

"Interpret, O riddler!" said I; "Gahagan Khan is no reader of puzzles—no prating mollah. Gujputi loves not words, but swords."

"Listen then, O Gujputi: you are in Holkar's power."

"I know it."

"You will die by the most horrible tortures to-morrow morning."

"I dare say."

"They will tear your teeth from your jaws, your nails from your fingers, and your eyes from your head."

"Very possibly."

"They will flay you alive, and then burn you."

"Well; they can't do any more."

"They will seize upon every man and woman in yonder fort"—it was not then taken!—"and repeat upon them the same tortures."

"Ha! Belinda! Speak—how can all this be avoided?"

"Listen. Gahagan loves the moon-face called Belinda."

"He does, Vizier, to distraction."

"Of what rank is he in the Koompani's army?"

"A captain."

"A miserable captain—oh, shame! Of what creed is he?"

"I am an Irishman, and a Catholic."

"But he has not been very particular about his religious duties?"

"Alas, no!"

"He has not been to his mosque for these twelve years?"

"'Tis too true."

"Hearken now, Gahagan Khan. His Highness Prince Holkar has sent me to thee. You shall have the moon-face for your wife—your second wife, that is;—the first shall be the incomparable Puttee Rooge, who loves you to madness;—with Puttee Rooge, who is the wife, you shall have the wealth and rank of Bobbachy Bahawder, of whom his Highness intends to get rid. You shall be second in command of his Highness's forces. Look, here is his commission signed with the celestial seal, and attested by the sacred names of the forty-nine Imaums. You have but to renounce your religion and your service, and all these rewards are yours."

He produced a parchment, signed as he said, and gave it to me (it was beautifully written in Indian ink: I had it for fourteen years, but a rascally valet, seeing it very dirty, washed it, forsooth, and washed off every bit of the writing). I took it calmly, and said, "This is a tempting offer. O Vizier, how long wilt thou give me to consider of it?"

After a long parley, he allowed me six hours, when I promised to give him an answer. My mind, however, was made up—as soon as he was gone, I threw myself on the sofa and fell asleep.

At the end of the six hours the Vizier came back: two people were with him; one, by his martial appearance, I knew to be Holkar, the other I did not recognise. It was about midnight.

"Have you considered?" said the Vizier, as he came to my couch.

"I have," said I, sitting up,—I could not stand, for my legs were tied, and my arms fixed in a neat pair of steel handcuffs. "I have," said I, "unbelieving dogs! I have. Do you think to pervert a Christian gentleman from his faith and honour? Ruffian blackamoors! do your worst; heap tortures on this body, they cannot last long. Tear me to pieces: after you have torn me into a certain number of pieces, I shall not feel it; and if I did, if each torture could last a life, if each limb were to feel the agonies of a whole body, what then? I would bear all—all—all— all—all—ALL!" My breast heaved—my form dilated—my eye flashed as I spoke these words. "Tyrants!" said I, "dulce et decorum est pro patria mori." Having thus clinched the argument, I was silent.

The venerable. Grand Vizier turned away; I saw a tear trickling down his cheeks.

"What a constancy!" said he. "Oh, that such beauty and such bravery should be doomed so soon to quit the earth!"

His tall companion only sneered and said, "AND BELINDA—?"

"Ha!" said I, "ruffian, be still!—Heaven will protect her spotless innocence. Holkar, I know thee, and thou knowest me too! Who, with his single sword, destroyed thy armies? Who, with his pistol, cleft in twain thy nose-ring? Who slew thy generals? Who slew thy elephants? Three hundred mighty beasts went forth to battle: of these I slew one hundred and thirty-five! Dog, coward, ruffian, tyrant, unbeliever! Gahagan hates thee, spurns thee, spits on thee!"

Holkar, as I made these uncomplimentary remarks, gave a scream of rage, and, drawing his scimitar, rushed on to despatch me at once (it was the very thing I wished for), when the third person sprang forward and, seizing his arm, cried -

"Papa! oh, save him!" It was Puttee Rooge! "Remember," continued she, "his misfortunes—remember, oh, remember my—love!"—and here she blushed, and putting one finger into her mouth, and hanging down her head, looked the very picture of modest affection.

Holkar sulkily sheathed his scimitar, and muttered, "'Tis better as it is; had I killed him now, I had spared him the torture. None of this shameless fooling, Puttee Rooge," continued the tyrant, dragging her away. "Captain Gahagan dies three hours from hence." Puttee Rooge gave one scream and fainted—her father and the Vizier carried her off between them; nor was I loth to part with her, for, with all her love, she was as ugly as the deuce.

They were gone—my fate was decided. I had but three hours more of life: so I flung myself again on the sofa, and fell profoundly asleep. As it may happen to any of my readers to be in the same situation, and to be hanged themselves, let me earnestly entreat them to adopt this plan of going to sleep, which I for my part have repeatedly found to be successful. It saves unnecessary annoyance, it passes away a great deal of unpleasant time, and it prepares one to meet like a man the coming catastrophe.

Three o'clock came: the sun was at this time making his appearance in the heavens, and with it came the guards, who were appointed to conduct me to the torture. I woke, rose, was carried out, and was set on the very white donkey on which Loll Mahommed was conducted through the camp after he was bastinadoed. Bobbachy Bahawder rode behind me, restored to his rank and state; troops of cavalry hemmed us in on all sides; my ass was conducted by the common executioner: a crier went forward, shouting out, "Make way for the destroyer of the faithful—he goes to bear the punishment of his crimes." We came to the fatal plain: it was the very spot whence I had borne away the elephant, and in full sight of the fort. I looked towards it. Thank Heaven! King George's banner waved on it still—a crowd were gathered on the walls—the men, the dastards who had deserted me—and women, too. Among the latter I thought I distinguished ONE who—O gods! the thought turned me sick—I trembled and looked pale for the first time.

"He trembles! he turns pale," shouted out Bobbachy Bahawder, ferociously exulting over his conquered enemy.

"Dog!" shouted I—(I was sitting with my head to the donkey's tail, and so looked the Bobbachy full in the face)—"not so pale as you looked when I felled you with this arm—not so pale as your women looked when I entered your harem!" Completely chop-fallen, the Indian ruffian was silent: at any rate, I had done for HIM.

We arrived at the place of execution. A stake, a couple of feet thick and eight high, was driven in the grass: round the stake, about seven feet from the ground, was an iron ring, to which were attached two fetters; in these my wrists were placed. Two or three executioners stood near, with strange-looking instruments: others were blowing at a fire, over which was a cauldron, and in the embers were stuck prongs and other instruments of iron.

The crier came forward and read my sentence. It was the same in effect as that which had been hinted to me the day previous by the Grand Vizier. I confess I was too agitated to catch every word that was spoken.

Holkar himself, on a tall dromedary, was at a little distance. The Grand Vizier came up to me—it was his duty to stand by, and see the punishment performed. "It is yet time!" said he.

I nodded my head, but did not answer.

The Vizier cast up to heaven a look of inexpressible anguish, and with a voice choking with emotion, said, "EXECUTIONER—DO—YOUR— DUTY!"

The horrid man advanced—he whispered sulkily in the ears of the Grand Vizier, "Guggly ka ghee, hum khedgeree," said he, "THE OIL DOES NOT BOIL YET—wait one minute." The assistants blew, the fire blazed, the oil was heated. The Vizier drew a few feet aside: taking a large ladle full of the boiling liquid, he advanced -

"Whish! bang, bang! pop!" the executioner was dead at my feet, shot through the head; the ladle of scalding oil had been dashed in the face of the unhappy Grand Vizier, who lay on the plain, howling. "Whish! bang! pop! Hurrah!—charge!—forwards!—cut them down!—no quarter!"

I saw—yes, no, yes, no, yes!—I saw regiment upon regiment of galloping British horsemen riding over the ranks of the flying natives. First of the host, I recognised, O Heaven! my AHMEDNUGGAR IRREGULARS! On came the gallant line of black steeds and horsemen; swift swift before them rode my officers in yellow—Glogger, Pappendick, and Stuffle; their sabres gleamed in the sun, their voices rung in the air. "D- them!" they cried, "give it them, boys!" A strength supernatural thrilled through my veins at that delicious music: by one tremendous effort, I wrested the post from its foundation, five feet in the ground. I could not release my hands from the fetters, it is true; but, grasping the beam tightly, I sprung forward—with one blow I levelled the five executioners in the midst of the fire, their fall upsetting the scalding oil-can; with the next, I swept the bearers of Bobbachy's palanquin off their legs; with the third, I caught that chief himself in the small of the back, and sent him flying on to the sabres of my advancing soldiers!

The next minute, Glogger and Stuffle were in my arms, Pappendick leading on the Irregulars. Friend and foe in that wild chase had swept far away. We were alone: I was freed from my immense bar; and ten minutes afterwards, when Lord Lake trotted up with his staff, he found me sitting on it.

"Look at Gahagan," said his Lordship. "Gentlemen, did I not tell you we should be sure to find him AT HIS POST?"

The gallant old nobleman rode on: and this was the famous BATTLE OF FURRUCKABAD, or SURPRISE OF FUTTYGHUR, fought on the 17th of November, 1804.

About a month afterwards, the following announcement appeared in the Boggleywollah Hurkaru and other Indian papers:-

"Married, on the 25th of December, at Futtyghur, by the Rev. Dr. Snorter, Captain Goliah O'Grady Gahagan, Commanding Irregular Horse, Ahmednuggar, to Belinda, second daughter of Major-General Bulcher, C.B. His Excellency the Commander-in-Chief gave away the bride; and, after a splendid dejeuner, the happy pair set off to pass the Mango season at Hurrygurrybang. Venus must recollect, however, that Mars must not always be at her side. The Irregulars are nothing without their leader."

Such was the paragraph—such the event—the happiest in the existence of G. O'G. G., M.H.E.I.C.S., C.I.H.A.

William Makepeace Thackeray, was born on July 18th, 1811 in Calcutta, then British India, where his father, Richmond Thackeray was the secretary to the Board of Revenue in the British East India Company. His mother, Anne Becher also worked for the British East India Company.

His father died in 1815, and his mother sent Thackeray to England the following year while she remained in India and would, sometime later, marry her childhood sweetheart. En-route to England the ship stopped for provisions on St. Helena. The Imprisoned Napoleon was pointed out to him by a servant with the words that he "eats three sheep every day, and all the little children he can lay hands on!"

Finally, back in England the young Thackeray was sent to school, initially in Southampton and Chiswick, before being moved to Charterhouse School. Charterhouse and Thackeray did not take to each other but the time became a valuable source for his later work "Slaughterhouse". Despite his less than respectful recalling of his time with them Charterhouse placed a monument in the chapel after his death.

In his final year at Charterhouse a troubling illness delayed his departure to attend Cambridge University. Over the course of his life Thackeray would suffer from ill health, much of it brought about for his fondness for "gluttling and gorging". Excess was something he could enjoy and for a man who stood some 6' 3" it would appear to the eye that, initially at least, his large frame could absorb much of that excess.

However, Thackeray's lazy attitude to completely mastering anything he set his mind too, especially where ambition for academia was involved, meant he departed Cambridge little more than a year after joining. He had however published two short works in University periodicals. As an author, he would have quite some impact on English literature in the years to come, so it seems difficult to reconcile that he felt no urgency to pursue writing at that time.

He now spent some time travelling across Europe stopping at both Paris, to study art, and to winter in Weimar. Back in London a final attempt was made on a professional career. This time studying law at Middle Temple. It lasted no more than a few months.

Now, having reached 21, he received his father's inheritance. It was a very substantial estate of 17,000 pounds, an enormous sum of money at the time. However, although Thackeray had youth he lacked a little in energy and certainly much financial experience. He funded not one but two newspapers, and neither was to prove successful. Gambling seemed enjoyable and certainly he had money to lose, which he did on a regular basis. Further investments in two soon-to-fail Indian banks quickly ensured little of his good fortune remained.

He now had to consider taking up yet another profession. Thackeray turned to art hoping that his studies in Paris would prove of benefit. Unfortunately, they did not. His ambivalent attitude continued until on August 20th, 1836 he married the 20-year-old, Isabella Gethin Shawe. It seemed to prove a turning point in many ways.

The marriage would produce three daughters; Anne Isabella in 1837, Jane, in 1838, who tragically died in infancy and Harriet Marian in 1840.

Now, as a husband and father, Thackeray seemed at last to understand his responsibilities to nurture and provide.

His early efforts at "writing for his life" were to establish his career as a foremost author. His main employment was with Fraser's Magazine, a sharp-witted and sharp-tongued conservative publication for which he produced art criticism, short fictional sketches, and who would also serialise two of his novels. He also found time, between 1837 and 1840 to review books for The Times and to make regular contributions to The Morning Chronicle and The Foreign Quarterly Review.

In his earliest works, which he wrote under various pseudonyms including; Charles James Yellowplush, Michael Angelo Titmarsh and George Savage Fitz-Boodle, he tended towards savagery in his attacks on high society, military prowess, the institution of marriage and hypocrisy.

Between May 1839 and February 1840 Fraser's published Catherine. Originally intended as a satire of the Newgate school of crime fiction, it ended up being more of a picaresque tale. Thackeray also began work on what would eventually become A Shabby Genteel Story.

However, Thackeray, having successfully found a career that he cared about and had the talent for, found that his personal life was about to descend into chaos. After the birth of her third child in 1840, Isabella, sank into depression. At first Thackeray, didn't think too much of it. He needed to work to earn an income to support his family and finding that Isabella was distracting both herself and him he realised he could get no work done at home and so spent more and more time away until finally, in September 1840, it dawned upon him how serious his wife's condition had become. Struck by guilt, he set out with his wife to Ireland. During the boat crossing she threw herself into the sea, but was thankfully pulled from the waters. Her mother who had little understanding of her daughter's illness was of little help and perhaps a hinderance. After four-weeks they returned to England. From November 1840 to February 1842 Isabella was in and out of professional care, as her condition waxed and waned.

Isabella eventually deteriorated into a permanent state of detachment. Thackeray desperately sought cures for her, but nothing worked, and she ended up in two different asylums in or near Paris until 1845, after which Thackeray took her back to England, where he installed her with a Mrs Bakewell at Camberwell. Despite her condition Isabella would outlive her husband by 3 decades.

After his wife's illness Thackeray became a de facto widower, never able to establish another permanent relationship.

In 1843, through his connection to the illustrator John Leech, whom he had met at Charterhouse, he began writing for the newly created magazine Punch, in which he published The Snob Papers, later collected as The Book of Snobs. Thackeray was a regular contributor to Punch until 1854.

Thackeray had earlier received some success with two travel books, The Paris Sketch Book and The Irish Sketch Book, the latter marked by hostility to Irish Catholics. The book appealed to British prejudices, and on that basis Thackeray now became Punch's Irish expert, often under the pseudonym Hibernis Hibernior. It was Thackeray's writings that were the basis for Punch's notoriously harsh, hostile and condescending depictions of the Irish during the devastating Irish Famine (1845–51).

As well as his regular columns and contributions Thackeray worked on his novels. In The Luck of Barry Lyndon, which was serialised in Fraser's in 1844, he explored the situation of an outsider trying to achieve status in high society, a theme he developed more successfully a few years later with Vanity Fair.

Thackeray achieved more recognition with his Snob Papers (serialised 1846/7, and published as a book in 1848), but the work that really established his fame was the novel Vanity Fair, which first appeared in serialised instalments beginning in January 1847.

Published as a book the novel had a slow start but eventually sales rose to 7,000 copies a month. Just as importantly, it was the book that everybody was talking about. Thackeray finally had a name that gained notice and was reviewed in journals such as the famed, and much sought after, Edinburgh Review.

The accolades and success also gave him a respite from writing everything in a manner that would help ensure income rather than literary respect. Even before Vanity Fair completed its serial run Thackeray had become a celebrity, sought after by the very lords and ladies whom he satirised. with the character of Becky Sharp, the artist's daughter who rises high by manipulating all around her.

Pendennis followed in 1849-50, but it was interrupted halfway through writing for 3 months by a severe illness. Some accounts say it was cholera. Pendennis is a semi-autobiographical bildungsroman that draws on, among other things, Thackeray's disappointments in college, his ambivalent relationship with his mother, and his insider's knowledge of the London publishing world.

This novel ran at the same time as Charles Dicken's David Copperfield, and their dual appearance brought about the first of many comparisons with Dickens. Thackeray, for his part, felt that he and Dickens were battling for supremacy, though he would never equal Dickens's popularity, except with the critics.

Interestingly the two were involved in a spat which became known as the "Garrick Club affair". Thackeray and Dickens had skirmished over the "Dignity of Literature" and had other slight disagreements but this literary quarrel caused a rift in their friendship that lasted almost until the end of Thackeray's life. The relationship was healed only in Thackeray's last months, through a surprise meeting and handshake on the steps of a London club. Thackeray had taken offense at some personal remarks in a column by Edmund Yates and demanded an apology, eventually taking the affair to the Garrick Club committee. Already upset with Thackeray for an indiscreet remark about his affair with Ellen Ternan, Dickens championed Yates, helping him to write letters both to Thackeray and, in his defense, to the club's committee. Despite the intervention of Dickens, Yates eventually lost the vote of the Club's members, but the quarrel was laid out for the public in journal articles and pamphlets. "What pains me most," Thackeray said at the time, "is that Dickens should have been his adviser, and next that I should have had to lay a heavy hand on a young man who, I take it, has been cruelly punished by the issue of the affair, and I believe is hardly aware of the nature of his own offence, and doesn't even now understand that a gentleman should resent the monstrous insult which he volunteered".

Aside from these quarrelsome, distracting literary disagreements and Isabella's on-going illness life was good for Thackeray. He was to remain as he put it "at the top of the tree," for the rest of his life. The works for which he is so well remembered; Vanity Fair and Barry Lyndon had established that but he continued to write and produce novels, stories, sketches and works profusely.

To remain at such a high level in both quality and quantity is somewhat surprising given the continuation and escalation of various illnesses which continued to haunt him.

With Isabella still unwell Thackeray did seek out other women, in particular Mrs Jane Brookfield. Despite his hopes, it always felt that he was pursuing her as she battled the problems of her own marriage and turned to Thackeray for comfort and support. A source for these relationships often came on the lecture tours of Great Britain and the United States which he now entertained. These tours gave the public a chance to see and hear their hero's and provided another valuable source of income for those invited to tour. Whilst in in New York he met the Baxter family. Sally, the eldest daughter, enchanted the novelist—as a number of vibrant, intelligent, beautiful young women had done before her—and she became the model for Ethel Newcome. He visited her on his second tour of the States when she was married to a South Carolina gentleman. His choosing of married women in the shape of both Jane and Sally was ill-advised and both relationships led nowhere but did take quite some time to disassemble and for reason to set in.

In 1852, The History of Henry Esmond was published as a 3-volume novel without first being serialised and in a special type meant to imitate the appearance of an eighteenth-century book. This was the most carefully planned of Thackeray's novels. The book was celebrated for its brilliance, and Thackeray recognized it as "the very best I can do". At the time, it caused a sensation thanks to its controversial ending, wherein the hero marries a woman who early in the novel seemed more like a "mother" to him.

The eighteenth-century held a great attraction for Thackeray and he had previously set both Barry Lyndon and Catherine there as well as the sequel to Esmond, The Virginians, which takes place in North America and includes George Washington as a character.

Thackeray had twice visited the United States on lecture tours during this period as well as given lectures in London on the English humorists of the eighteenth century, and on the first four Hanoverian monarchs. The latter were published in a book as The Four Georges.

Interestingly Thackeray also decided that Politics was something he could more than dabble in. In Oxford he stood as an independent for Parliament. He was narrowly beaten by Cardwell, a politician who was substituted for the man Thackeray thought he was going to run against, although Thackeray's advocacy of entertainment on the Sabbath would have done little to help his campaign. Even so the margin of his defeat was only 1,070 votes, to Thackeray's 1,005.

In 1860 Thackeray became editor of the newly established Cornhill Magazine, a role he never felt truly comfortable in, preferring to contribute as a columnist on the Roundabout Papers. However, the financial compensation was by all accounts quite extraordinary. The Cornhill began its history with a record circulation and a number of distinguished contributors swayed onboard by Thackeray's reputation. It was in the Cornhill that he serialised his last complete novel, The Adventures of Philip in 1861-62. (After his death, the incomplete Denis Duval would also appear there in 1864).

After two years as editor he stepped down, primarily to concentrate on writing novels again. A piece he wrote for the Cornhill at this time "Thorns in the Cushion," one of The Roundabout Papers, fondly assembles the pains he felt in rejecting manuscripts on the one hand and receiving criticism of the magazine on the other. It seemed a good time to move on.

Thackeray's health had worsened during the 1850s and he was plagued by a recurring stricture of the urethra that laid him up for days at a time. He also felt that he had lost much of his creative impetus. He worsened matters by excessively eating and drinking, and avoiding exercise, though he enjoyed horseback-riding. He has been described as "the greatest literary glutton who ever lived". Indeed, his main activity apart from writing was eating and drinking and many of his stories include elaborate scenes and themes on his fondness for them.

On December 23rd, 1863, William Makepeace Thackeray, after returning from dining out and before dressing for bed, suffered a massive stroke. He was found dead on his bed the following morning. He was only fifty-two.

His death was entirely unexpected, and shocked family, friends and indeed the entire Nation.

It is said that at his funeral service thousands of mourners turned out to witness his passing. He was buried on December 29th at Kensal Green Cemetery, London.

William Makepeace Thackeray – A Concise Bibliography

The Yellowplush Papers (1837)
Catherine (1839–40)
A Shabby Genteel Story (1840)
Second Funeral of Napoleon (1841)
The Irish Sketchbook (1843)
The Luck of Barry Lyndon (1844)
Notes of a Journey from Cornhill to Grand Cairo (1846)
Mrs. Perkins's Ball (1846), under the name M. A. Titmarsh
Stray Papers: Being Stories, Reviews, Verses, and Sketches (1821-1847)
The Book of Snobs (1848)
Vanity Fair (1848)
Pendennis (1848–1850)
Rebecca and Rowena (1850)
The Paris Sketchbook (1840)
Men's Wives (1852)
The History of Henry Esmond (1852)
The English Humorists of the Eighteenth Century (1853)
The Newcomes (1855)
The Rose and the Ring (1855)
The Virginians (1857–1859)
Lovel the Widower (1860)
Four Georges (1860-1861)
The Adventures of Philip (1862)
Roundabout Papers (1863)
Denis Duval (1864)
The English Humorists of the eighteenth century: A Series of Six Lectures (1867)
Ballads (1869)
Burlesques (1869)

The Orphan of Pimlico (1876)

Thackeray wrote a numerous number of articles for magazines and the like as well as contributing many picture sketches to articles and his own books. Many were then collected and published together. We have listed his major works only for this bibliography.